THE SUICIDE SQUAD:
TARGETS FOR THE FLAMING ARROW
AND OTHER STORIES

ACE G-MAN

TARGETS FOR THE
FLAMING ARROW
AND OTHER STORIES

By Emile C. Tepperman

POPULAR PUBLICATIONS • 2023

PUBLISHING HISTORY

"Move Over, Death!" originally appeared in the October 1942 (Vol. 18, No. 2) issue of *Ace G-Man Stories* magazine. "Targets for the Flaming Arrow" originally appeared in the December 1942 (Vol. 10, No. 3) issue of *Ace G-Man Stories* magazine. "Blood, Sweat and Bullets" originally appeared in the February 1943 (Vol. 10, No. 4) issue of *Ace G-Man Stories* magazine. "The Suicide Squad and The Twins of Death" originally appeared in the April 1943 (Vol. 11, No. 1) issue of *Ace G-Man Stories* magazine. Copyright 2023 by Argosy Communications, Inc. All rights reserved.

MOVE OVER, DEATH!

CHAPTER 1
STRICTLY SOLO

O N APRIL 4, the Dutch cargo vessel, *Mynheer Vanderdonk*, left New York and joined a convoy for Melbourne. Its freight consisted of medium tank parts, .37 mm. guns, thirty thousand Garand rifles, two million rounds of Garand ammunition, and six Airacobras ready to assemble.

While being loaded, the *Mynheer Vanderdonk* had undergone a fine-comb inspection by U.S. Army officers. Yet on her fourth day out, she exploded in mid-ocean, and went down with all hands.

Since the only possible solution to this disaster was that a time bomb of some sort had been placed in her hold by a saboteur working as a stevedore, the F.B.I. assigned one of its agents to the job of working on that particular pier, which was operated by the Pearl Steamship Company. They gave him a card in the Longshoremen's Union, and provided him with a completely new personality.

He reported for work on April 10th. That evening, when he returned to the furnished room he had hired a block from the waterfront, a bomb exploded almost in his face, killing him instantly.

The next day, twenty-four F.B.I. men were taken off regular duty, and assigned to the task of investigating each and every one of the employees on the Pearl Steamship Company Pier. They found two enemy aliens, one ex-convict, and one member of the

German-American Bund. Those four were taken into custody on suspicion of sabotage and murder. The loading of the next ship, the Russian freighter, *Byalostok*, continued. The vigilance of the inspectors was not relaxed. Yet, four days after she sailed, an explosion occurred in the after hold of the *Byalostok*, and

Johnny was shooting with one hand, while slashing the picture with the other.

she sank so swiftly that not a single member of the crew had a chance for his life.

The F.B.I. put another undercover man on the pier. They arranged with Hugo Savage, the boss of the Savage Stevedoring Company, to make this man a timekeeper, so that he would be in a position to check everyone entering or leaving the pier.

This second undercover man was given two assistants.

One of them worked in the hold of the vessel then being loaded, at the delicate task of stowing the cargo. The other worked on the deck, supervising the operation of one of the winches. They all had union cards, and their identity as F.B.I. agents was kept secret. When the next boat—the Panamanian steamer, *Rosario*—was fully loaded, the three G-men were ready to swear that there was nothing in her hold that could possibly explode.

Yet the *Rosario* met the same fate as the *Mynheer Vanderdonk* and the *Byalostok!*

And on the same day that the *Rosario* exploded at sea, all three of the G-men were killed. One was stabbed to death in the Waterside Tavern, a bar and grille opposite the pier. The other two were shot to death with a high-powered rifle as they left their hotel.

It was just about this time that Kerrigan, Murdoch and Klaw returned to the States from Valparaiso, where they had destroyed the Zambetta organization. When they reached Washington, they got a summons to report to the Director of the Federal Bureau of Investigation.

"You're entitled to a vacation, boys," the Director told them grimly. "But there's a job in New York that I don't dare assign to anybody else. Judging by what's happened in the past, it looks like certain death for anyone who tackles it."

He didn't have to say any more. "Forget the vacation," Stephen Klaw told him, speaking for Kerrigan and Murdoch as well. THE DIRECTOR smiled. "I knew that would be your answer," he said. "I've already got you three berths on the midnight plane to New York. As for the rest, I leave it entirely in your hands." He explained the situation in detail, then asked, "How are you going to handle it?"

"One of us will go in as a stevedore," Stephen Klaw said, "the same as those other agents. He'll be the bait. We'll assume that the enemy has some means of putting the finger on our men, so we'll take it for granted that there'll be an attempt to kill him. The other two will cover him. In that way we may catch the killer—and the killer may lead us to the nest."

The Director said reluctantly, "It's dangerous, but there's no choice. I'll arrange by phone with Hugo Savage to have one job ready. Which one of you will take it?"

"I will," Steve Klaw said.

"Nix," exclaimed Johnny Kerrigan, standing up. "Nothing doing, Shrimp!"

Klaw grinned. He took a coin out of his pocket. "All right, we'll toss—"

Dan Murdoch said, "Nuts, Shrimp. You've won every toss that I can remember. I think you have a phony coin there—two tails or two heads. We won't toss for *this* one. You're automatically out!"

"How come?"

Murdoch's eyes twinkled. "Stand up!" he said.

Steve complied. Murdoch nodded to Kerrigan, and they both stood up too. They went and stood on either side of Stephen Klaw. Although Klaw was five foot seven and a half, Kerrigan and Murdoch towered over him like giants.

"See why, *Shrimp?*" Murdoch demanded, looking down his nose at him. "This is a stevedore's job. What kind of stevedore do you think you'd look like?"

"This is one time you don't cop the gravy, Shrimp!" said Kerrigan.

Klaw scowled angrily. He glanced at the Director, who chuckled. "It looks as if they've got you this time, Steve."

"Okay, mopes," Klaw said disgustedly. "You win!"

Murdoch grinned, and produced a coin. "All right, Johnny," he said to Kerrigan. "You and I toss."

Kerrigan shook his head. "Sorry, Dan. It's got to be me." He appealed to the Director. "What do you say, sir? Don't I look like a stevedore?"

Powerfully built, with massive shoulders, there was no denying his contention.

Murdoch shrugged resignedly. "I guess you and I'll have to ride herd on him, Shrimp!"

Klaw nodded. "All right, Johnny," he said. "It's your show. We'll be around, though. Suppose we contact you at that Waterside Tavern? That's where they killed one of our men. Maybe they'll come to the well once too often!"

And so it was that John Kerrigan reported for work as a stevedore at the Pearl Steamship Company pier at eight o'clock the next morning.

CHAPTER 2
"LIQUIDATE THEM!"

H UGO SAVAGE, the boss stevedore, met Johnny Kerrigan at the gate, and passed him through the guard.

"We're pretty well protected here, as you see," he told Johnny. "Nobody gets in who doesn't belong."

Savage was a big man in his early fifties, chunky and pugnacious. "I came to this country forty years ago," he said, as he led Johnny Kerrigan to the timekeeper's shack. Then he added, almost challengingly, "I came from Germany. But don't get any wrong ideas—I'm an American citizen and I hate everything that Hitler stands for. I feel worse about these ships going down than anybody else, because my men loaded them. I want to get to the bottom of it, and I'll do everything I can to help you."

Inside the timekeeper's shack, a baldheaded man wearing an eyeshade was seated at a desk.

"Lou Moynes, my chief timekeeper," Hugo Savage introduced. "Lou, this is a new man. John Kerrigan. Start his time now. I'm putting him to work in A Hold."

Moynes rose and nodded to Johnny. He got a pad, and wrote the name down.

"Kerrigan?" he said. "I don't recall the name. Have you ever worked for us before?"

"No," said Johnny.

"But you've done stevedoring?"

"No," Johnny said again. "I never loaded a ship in my life."

Lou Moynes looked at him sharply. "You mean, you've got *no* experience?"

"That's right," Johnny said, grinning. He winked at Hugo Savage, who was making frantic motions to him, behind Moynes' back.

The timekeeper turned around to Savage. "How can we put him on?" he demanded. "We can't use him—"

"It's all right," Kerrigan interrupted. "I won't get in your way. I'm from the F.B.I."

If he had said he was from Mars, he could not have startled Moynes any more. The man's mouth dropped open, and he stared at Johnny.

Hugo Savage looked angry and puzzled. "See here, Kerrigan," he protested. "I thought this was to be a secret between you and me. I didn't even tell Moynes who you were. Good Lord, man, do you want to advertise that you're from the F.B.I.? Do you want to *invite* them to kill you?"

"That," Johnny Kerrigan said happily, "is exactly what I want to do."

SAVAGE THREW up his hands. "The man is crazy!"

Lou Moynes blinked, took off his eyeshade. There was a sharp line across his forehead where the eyeshade had pressed against the skin.

"If your name is Kerrigan," he said slowly, "you must be one of the Suicide Squad."

"That's what they call us," Johnny said.

Moynes sighed. "I can see why. You couldn't be taking a more certain way to commit suicide. Why, it's like—like getting right into bed with death!"

Kerrigan grinned. "I'll ask him to move over, then."

Moynes shrugged, and made out a slip for him. "I've read a lot about you and Murdoch and Klaw. But I thought the stories were exaggerated. They said you never got routine assignments, but were always kept in reserve for jobs where the chances of coming out alive were small. They say you three always go around as if you were *looking* for death."

He sighed, and gave Johnny the slip he had made out. "This will pass you on to the ship. I have to take a picture of you, and have a badge made. But I almost think it'll be a waste of time. You'll probably be dead before the picture is developed!"

He got out a large box camera with a flash-gun attachment, and snapped a picture of Johnny.

"I'll take it across the street and have it developed. The badge will be ready by lunch time, so you can go out and come back past the guard at one o'clock—if you live that long!"

Kerrigan grinned, took the slip, and followed Hugo Savage out of the shack. Savage led him out on the dock, threading the way among high piled crates of machinery. The winches were creaking and men were working, shouting and sweating on the high deck of the ship, as crate after crate was raised then lowered into the hold.

"For God's sake," Savage begged, stopping at the gangplank and taking Johnny's arm, "do me a favor. Don't tell everybody you're from the F.B.I. Give yourself half a chance!"

"Listen," said Johnny. "Murdoch and Klaw and I don't work that way. We don't believe in pussy-footing around. This pier has been investigated constantly, and nothing has been turned up. We could keep investigating for another year, and the ships could keep on sinking. But we have a better way. We'll bring the enemy out in the open."

Savage shook his head helplessly, and led Johnny up on the deck. He introduced him to Tony Pellagi, the foreman of A Hold.

"This is Kerrigan, a new man," he said. "Show him the ropes."

"Any experience?" Pellagi demanded. "You know anything about stowing?"

"Not a thing," said Johnny. "I'm not a stevedore by trade. I'm a G-man."

Hugo Savage groaned. "I'm going," he said. "I don't want to be around when you get killed." He put his hand on Pellagi's shoulder. "Keep an eye on him, Tony. I think he's crazy."

"Me, too," said Pellagi. He shrugged. "But it ain't my funeral. You can hang around and watch for a while. Then I'll send you down in the hold. And you better have eyes in the back of your head down there!"

BACK IN the timekeeper's shack, Lou Moynes was staring out of the window, across the busy dock, at the big figure of Johnny Kerrigan on the deck of the boat. There was a peculiar, baffled expression on Moynes' face. He kept tugging at his eyeshade. He waited till Hugo Savage returned to the shack, then he picked up the camera.

"I better take this over and have it printed," he said. "We might as well get him the badge."

Savage nodded absently and Moynes went out with the camera. Just outside the gate, he almost collided with a slim, youthful looking chap who was peddling razor blades. It seemed that he had been trying to get permission to enter the pier but the guard had turned him away.

The young fellow buttonholed Lou Moynes, displaying his open valise. "How about some blades, mister?" he demanded. "Best blades in the country. Guaranteed to cut your throat with one swipe. Come on, you know you can use razor blades. Buy a package!"

Moynes was about to push past, but the young fellow got in front of him. "Now listen, mister, you can't afford to pass this up. Fifty blades for a dime."

The timekeeper stopped. "Fifty for a dime? What do you do, steal them?"

"I'm just trying to work my way through college."

"College? What college?"

"Barber's college!" the young fellow said triumphantly.

Moynes chuckled in spite of himself. He picked up a package from the valise and took a dime out of his pocket.

"Wait a minute," said the young salesman. "That's an open package that I use for samples. Here's a fresh one, never been opened."

Moynes put down the first package and took the other one. He paid the dime over, and continued on across the street toward a photographer's shop, in whose window was displayed a large sign:

PASSPORT AND BADGE PHOTOS
WHILE YOU WAIT

He didn't see two things which would have interested him greatly. He didn't see how the young salesman slipped the discarded package of blades into a cellophane envelope, handling it carefully, so as not to disturb the fingerprints which Lou Moynes had left upon it.

Neither did he see the tall handsome man in the station wagon parked fifty feet down the street, who was crouching in the back of the car with a camera equipped with a telefoto lens, and who snapped Moynes' picture just as he moved away from the razor blade salesman.

Had he seen either of those two things, he might not have continued across the street.

He entered the photographer's store, and glanced around swiftly to make sure there were no other customers. A thin man came from the rear, saw who it was, and grunted.

Moynes handed the camera to the thin man.

"We have another G-man!" he said swiftly. "This one is a fool. He makes it easy for us. We don't even have to check on him. He announces to everyone who he is!"

The thin man smiled crookedly. "These Americans!" he said. "They are mad fools." He took the camera.

"This one is no fool," said Moynes. "He is Kerrigan, one of the Suicide Squad. You will have to tell von Rieber that he must be liquidated quickly. Make two pictures, one for the badge, and one for von Rieber—"

He stopped abruptly. The front door had opened, and the young razor blade salesman entered. They could not tell whether or not he had heard anything.

"Hi!" said the salesman. "Did you know you gave me a quarter instead of a dime? Here's your change."

He came over, his valise hanging open by a strap from his shoulder, and offered Moynes fifteen cents.

Moynes frowned. "I am sure I gave you a dime."

The salesman grinned. He looked utterly youthful and harmless, like a kid just out of college.

"Honesty is the best policy," he said. "Here's your fifteen cents. Or would you like to take some more blades?"

"All right, all right," Moynes said.

"They're three for a quarter."

Moynes took the other two packages, and then the salesman tried to make a sale to the thin man, but he was waved away. **THEY WATCHED** him go out, and then the thin man said tightly, "Do you think he heard you mention von Rieber?"

"I don't know, Braun. I am beginning to wonder. He sells these blades very cheap. It is suspicious. And I am sure that I only gave him a dime. He invented the excuse to follow me in here!"

Braun's eyes became very narrow. "Von Rieber feared that the Suicide Squad might be assigned to this job. It may be that this salesman is another one of them. We must not take chances. He must die. It is the only safe way."

Moynes agreed. "It is best that he should be liquidated."

Braun took the camera and went back to the dark room in the rear, while Moynes paced up and down, glancing out the show window every once in a while to make sure that the salesman had not gone away.

At last, Braun came out with two damp prints, each about two inches square.

"All right," he said. "I phoned von Rieber. He says that he will handle everything. He is sending a liquidation committee to take care of that salesman outside. And the other, Kerrigan, will be put out of the way at the Waterside Tavern. See that he goes there tonight."

"That will be easy," said Moynes. "I'll have him there at nine o'clock."

Braun gave him the two pictures. "One is for the badge. The other must go to the Waterside Tavern. Number Thirteen will do the job there, and he will pick up the picture from Fuerken, so that he will know his man."

"Have we a messenger to take this picture to the Waterside Tavern?"

Braun nodded. "Number Forty-two is outside. Have him take it in. In view of that salesman's presence, it is best that you do not go there yourself."

Moynes nodded. He took his camera and the two pictures, and went out.

In the street, there was a small, white-painted ice-cream cart, with a uniformed attendant. Moynes walked down to the cart and bought an ice-cream sandwich. He slipped one of the photographs to the attendant.

"Take this to Fuerken in the Waterside Tavern, at once!" he said. "Von Rieber's orders!"

The man nodded.

Moynes crossed the street, eating the ice-cream sandwich. He saw with satisfaction that the young salesman was still outside the pier gate. Moynes smiled at him.

"Stay here, my young friend," he advised. "I shall tell the men inside of your bargains. Wait here until their rest period and you will make many sales."

"Thanks," said the salesman. "I'll remember you in my will."

Moynes chuckled. "You expect to die so young then, my friend?"

"Any minute now!" the salesman told him.

Moynes chuckled again, and went inside the gate. He made his way back to the timekeeper's shack, still chuckling.

But out in the street, the young razor blade man was watching the ice-cream cart. He saw the attendant trundle it down the block, stop in front of the Waterside Tavern, and hurry in. His eyes became narrow, coldly gray. He turned his head and exchanged an almost imperceptible signal with the dark-haired man in the station wagon. Then he began to move down the street toward the Waterside Tavern.

It was just then that the "liquidation committee" arrived.

CHAPTER 3
THE SUICIDE SQUAD
TAKES OVER

THE "LIQUIDATION committee" consisted of three men in an inconspicuous-looking car. Two men sat in front, and one in back. They were grim-faced men, with a strangely fanatic ruthlessness in their eyes, and the stiff, unbending attitude of storm troopers. As the car swung into the street in front of the pier, they spied the salesman crossing toward the Waterside Tavern.

"There he is, Schlieffer!" the driver exclaimed, nudging the one beside him. "That is the one who was described to us! See the valise hanging from the strap around his neck!"

"Ach!" said Schlieffer, cuddling a revolver in his hand. "It is almost too good to be true! We do not even need to shoot him. Run him down, Heinrich. Quick!"

"Jawohl!" Heinrich's big red hands gripped the wheel; his foot pressed all the way down on the accelerator. The car leaped forward, heading straight for the unsuspecting salesman, like a projectile fired from a heavy gun.

The man in the rear leaned forward eagerly to watch the sport.

"See how he walks to his doom!" he exclaimed. "Now he turns his head. He sees us! He understands. It is useless to try to run. He cannot escape! *Ai-eee....*"

The last was an expression of intense amazement and sudden terror. For there was a loud explosion, and the right rear tire blew out.

None of those three knew what had caused the blowout, for they had not noticed the station wagon they had passed, nor had they seen the dark-haired man in that station wagon draw a revolver from his shoulder holster and snap a single shot at their tire.

But it wouldn't have done them any good to know the cause of the blowout. The car, racing more than sixty miles an hour, slewed to the right, tipping far over to one side. The driver fought the wheel frantically for an instant, then it was ripped from his hands as if by a tornado. The car hurtled the sidewalk, went over on its side with a terrible crash, and jammed up against the pier gate with a terrific crash. The hood folded like an accordion, driving the heavy motor back into the tonneau, crushing the two men in front. The top buckled down on the head of the man in the rear, and then a vivid sheet of fire sizzled upward from the gas tank, enveloping the car and its occupants.

The street was suddenly filled with horrified spectators as men ran from the dock and from the stores on the opposite side, and stood gaping, at a safe distance. No one dared to approach, for fear that the tank would explode. But by some miracle, it did not. However, by the time the fire apparatus got there, the wrecked car was nothing but a heap of molten metal.

AT THE fringe of the crowd, the tall, dark-haired man and the young razor blade salesman stood alongside each other, exchanging solemn glances.

"That was as beautiful a piece of shooting as I ever saw, mope," said the young salesman.

"It wasn't bad, Shrimp," said Dan Murdoch. "Even if I say

17

so myself." He paused, then added, "It looks like you've drawn blood with those razor blades of yours. How did you do it so fast?"

"It's a knack," Stephen Klaw said modestly.

"Where do we go from here?" Murdoch demanded.

"The Waterside Tavern," Klaw told him. "That bird with the camera slipped something to the ice-cream man, who hot-footed it into the Tavern. My guess would be that he had Kerrigan's picture developed and printed in that photographer's shop, and then gave one of the prints to the ice-cream man. It would seem that Johnny is to be put on the spot."

"Well," said Murdoch, "what are we waiting for?"

Unobserved, they backed out of the crowd, and went into the Waterside Tavern. The lettering on the window informed the public that this was Fuerken's Waterside Tavern; Adolph Fuerken, Prop.

There were no customers inside. Any who might have been there had hurried out to see the accident. In fact, the bartender had come out also, and he was standing in the thick of the crowd, gaping at the blazing car.

Murdoch and Klaw stepped into the empty barroom, and at once heard an excited voice speaking somewhere in the rear. They tiptoed to the back, and peered through the open doorway of the back room. A thick-set man, the back of whose neck was very red, was blubbering into the mouthpiece of a wall telephone. He was so excited that he was speaking partly in English and partly in German.

"No, no, Major von Rieber," he was saying. "I tell you, *doch,* they did not get that salesman. Something went wrong. Schlieffer and Heinrich and Hans are dead. *Todt.* They must have had a blow-out. *Ja, ja,* it was a blow-out. I came to the door just when the tire went. It was terrible. The car smashed into the pier gate. There *ist* nothing left but bones and ashes."

He stopped talking, and listened to the voice at the other end. At the doorway, Murdoch and Klaw exchanged significant glances. They had learned one thing—the name of the evil genius behind the organization: von Rieber. Major von Rieber, with whom they had locked horns more than once before America had entered the war. In those days, von Rieber had operated with impunity, taking advantage of our liberal laws to work for the destruction of the United States. But when war was declared, von Rieber had disappeared. Some had thought that he had left the country for South America, as Zambetta had done. But the Director of the F.B.I. had been almost certain that von Rieber was only lying low, waiting till the time was ripe to strike.

And this was indeed the time to strike. With the United Nations clamoring for more and more munitions, ships had become more valuable than guns. To strike at the United Nations' shipping facilities was a more telling blow than the destruction of an army corps. For the guns and tanks and fighter planes which we were turning out in ever-increasing quantities would do no good on the docks of America. Without ships to take them to the far-flung battle fronts of the world, they might as well never have been made.

Fuerken was talking again, evidently in reply to something that von Rieber had said over the phone.

"Jawohl, Herr Major. The other—that Kerrigan—he comes here tonight at nine? Number Thirteen will do it, you say? Very good, *Herr* Major. I will see to it that Number Thirteen makes his escape afterward. Do not worry, *Herr* Major. It shall be done as you say. And I will watch for the salesman of razor blades. As you say, he must be another of the accursed Suicide Squad...."

He talked for a moment longer, and then hung up.

When he turned around, he looked into the big black muzzle of Dan Murdoch's revolver.

"Tut, tut, *Herr* Fuerken," said Murdoch. "Don't let your jaw hang like that. Close your mouth. You don't want to catch flies, do you?"

FUERKEN'S MOUTH closed with a snap. He took one look at Klaw's open valise, and groaned.

"Ach! The Suicide Squad!"

Klaw grinned. He stepped behind him, took the receiver off the hook, and called the telephone company's chief operator. He talked for a moment, then hung up glumly.

"It was a call from a dial phone," he said to Murdoch. "They can't trace it."

Murdoch moved the muzzle of his revolver a little closer to Fuerken's mouth. "Do you care to talk, *Herr* Fuerken?" he asked gently.

The red-necked man was shaking like a jelly-fish. "T-talk? About—about what?"

"About von Rieber," Murdoch said. "This is war, Fuerken. And you're a spy. You know the penalty, don't you?"

"No, no!" Fuerken exclaimed. "America does not shoot spies. It puts them in prison."

Murdoch poked the gun muzzle against his head. "Here's one spy that's going to be shot right now—unless he talks fast. We want to know where to find von Rieber."

"I swear to you that I do not know!"

"You lie. You just told von Rieber that you'd help Number Thirteen escape after he kills Kerrigan. How can you help him escape if you don't know where to send him?"

"It is the truth. I do not know! None of us knows where to find von Rieber. When it is a matter of communicating with him, we call Braun, in the photographer's shop. He knows. The way I help our man to escape is to take him around the back, to Braun's shop. In the alley, a car will be waiting. But that is all I know. I swear—"

Murdoch waved him to silence. He looked inquiringly at Klaw.

Steve nodded. "Hold him here. I'll go and get Braun."

A couple of minutes later, Steve returned. "The photographer's shop is closed. Braun is gone."

Murdoch said, "We can't give up. We've got to get von Rieber."

"The only way we'll do it, is to let that Number Thirteen make his attempt on Johnny, and then to check on where he's taken."

They looked at each other, while Fuerken stood and trembled.

"All right," Murdoch said at last. "We'll do it. Johnny would want us to."

"In that case," said Steve, "we'll have to sort of take over in here."

"I never ran a saloon before," Murdoch said doubtfully.

"I once tended bar when I went to college," Klaw told him. "I guess I can do it again."

Murdoch waved the gun at Fuerken. "Lie down in that corner. You're going to be there for quite a while, until nine o'clock. You might as well make yourself comfortable."

Fuerken hastened to obey.

Steve got an apron from a peg, put it on. "I'll send the bartender in here when he comes back," he said. "You can ride herd on them while I serve the customers."

"Don't drink too much beer," Murdoch told him.

CHAPTER 4
THE BLACK HAT

AT NINE o'clock, Johnny Kerrigan walked into Fuerken's Waterside Tavern, blinked when he saw the bartender, and suppressed a grin. He ordered beer.

When he finished it, it seemed that he had nothing better to do than to stare down into the bottom of his empty glass. Actually he was reading the message written in indelible pencil on the bit of paper which was stuck, face up, to the underside of the glass. It said:

Watch your back, mope!

Johnny grinned into the glass. Then he glanced down the bar to where Stephen Klaw, with an apron tied around his middle, was giving a good imitation of a kid bartender on his first job.

22

Johnny caught Steve's attention, and let one eyelid droop almost imperceptibly. Klaw was busy serving whiskey to a couple of stevedores, and he gave Johnny a cold stare in response to the wink.

Kerrigan took the hint. He didn't know just how the situation shaped up. And he didn't know how Stephen Klaw came to be tending bar here. But he knew that Klaw hadn't placed the warning note in the bottom of the glass without good reason. So he concentrated his attention on the mirror behind the bar, which afforded a good view of what went on behind him.

And that was how he saw the little man with his hat in his hand.

It was just an old black felt hat, which he held in front of him. He'd got up from one of the booths, and he was coming up to the bar directly behind Johnny. He had a thin and scrawny neck, and he moved with an oozing motion which gave the impression that he might be double-jointed. His hair was black and matted over his forehead, and his eyes were very small and very black too. They were fixed on Kerrigan's broad-shouldered back, and the little man was moving forward as if with a fixed purpose.

Johnny tensed, both hands on the bar. The stevedores on either side of him were engrossed in their liquor and the conversation, and no one but Kerrigan was paying any attention to the little man with the matted hair and his hat in his hands.

The little fellow was close behind Johnny now, and he looked over into the mirror, to see if Johnny had noticed him. Kerrigan quickly swung his eyes away, and glanced down the bar toward

Klaw. Steve was drawing a beer, but he wasn't looking at the tap. He was looking at the little man behind Kerrigan.

Kerrigan smiled thinly. As long as Steve had his eyes on the fellow, Johnny didn't have to worry. But he stood tense nevertheless, on the balls of his feet, ready to swing into action in a split-second.

And then he got the warning flicker from Steve, just the flutter of an eyelid, but it was enough. Johnny's eyes swung back to the mirror, and he glimpsed the little man driving in toward him, thrusting his hat forward so that it would strike Johnny's back somewhere between the shoulder blades.

Kerrigan moved like an adagio dancer on greased bearings. He sidestepped to the left, bumping into the man next to him at the bar. At the same time, he swivelled on his left foot.

The little man had thrust the hat all the way forward now, and the knife which was concealed behind it gouged into the mahogany front of the bar, piercing the crown of the hat. It missed Johnny Kerrigan by a fraction of an inch.

The little killer blinked his eyes, staring at the knife, no doubt wondering how he had missed. He didn't get a chance to wonder long, because Johnny Kerrigan's big hand got a grip around the back of his neck, and Johnny just pushed him forward sharply, so that his forehead struck against the edge of the bar. The little killer sagged under the impact. The stevedores on either side of Johnny turned to stare.

"Hey, what's goin' on?" one of them growled.

KERRIGAN GRINNED, and pointed to the knife, which

was still quivering in the wood, its bone handle flickering in the light.

"Just a guy trying to stab me," said Johnny. "Forget it."

"Hah!" said the stevedore. "The dirty little scum! He tried to knife you in the back! Break his neck—"

"Nix," Johnny interrupted. "Why get sore about it? It wasn't you he was trying to stab. It was me."

"Sure, sure," said the big fellow, while several of the others crowded around. "But we can't have rats like him running loose. What'd he try to kill you for, anyway?"

"He was jealous," Johnny said. "He wanted my girl."

"You ought to teach him a lesson—"

"All right," Johnny agreed. "I'll take him in the back room, and give him a working over."

"Good idea!" the stevedores chorussed. And one of them added, "Fix the rat up so he won't never want to use a knife on anybody else. That's not the way Americans fight."

Kerrigan grinned. "I'll teach him the Star-Spangled Banner!"

He picked the semi-conscious knife-man up by the scruff of the neck, and carried him, without apparent effort, down toward the rear. Dressed in rough clothing, with knee-high boots and a turtle-neck sweater, Johnny looked just like any of the stevedores in the place, and they naturally accepted him as one of their own.

As he passed the spot where Steve Klaw was standing behind the bar, Steve gave him a solemn, owlish look. "The back room is empty," Steve said. "Go right in. And don't worry about making noise. We won't hear a thing." He looked around at the gathered stevedores, and winked. "Will we, boys?"

"Hell, no!" they shouted. "The more that rat yells, the less we'll hear!"

"What about Fuerken?" one of them asked. "Where is he? He won't like it. What's happened to him? This is the first time I seen the place at night, without Fuerken being around. And Julius, his bartender—where's he?"

"Fuerken isn't feeling good tonight," Steve Klaw said. "And neither is Julius. I'm sort of taking over."

He moved down toward the rear, took out a key, and unlocked the door of the back room. He opened it only wide enough to admit Johnny Kerrigan with his burden.

"Nice work so far, mope," he whispered as Kerrigan passed him. "Don't take too long inside. There's big stuff on for tonight."

Johnny nodded grimly, and stepped into the back room. Steve locked the door after him.

Inside, Kerrigan dropped his burden on the floor and looked around. He saw just why *Herr* Fuerken and his bartender, Julius, weren't "feeling good tonight."

Julius the bartender was lying on his face on the floor in one corner of the room, and *Herr* Fuerken was in the same position in another corner. Seated at the table, coolly sipping a Pepsi Cola, was Dan Murdoch.

MURDOCH LOOKED as darkly handsome and immaculate as ever, and he was smiling and talking pleasantly to Fuerken.

"Hi, Johnny," said Murdoch. "Put down your parcel and squat." He glanced at the slumped figure of the little knife-man. "You did all right."

"Not bad," said Johnny. He dropped the knife-man carelessly

on the floor, and sat down opposite Dan. He picked up Dan's bottle, and took a deep gulp of the Pepsi Cola.

"What goes on?" he demanded. "How come you and the shrimp have gone in the saloon business?"

Murdoch grinned. "We just took over for tonight. We sort of used you as bait, to catch that little knife-man of yours. We hope he'll lead us to von Rieber."

"Von Rieber!" exclaimed Johnny. "So he's in this!"

"And how!" said Murdoch. He proceeded swiftly to detail the situation to Kerrigan. By the time he had finished, Stephen Klaw opened the door and stepped into the back room.

"How's the saloon business, Shrimp?" Kerrigan asked.

"Rotten," Steve told him. "I told the customers the beer was all gone, so they picked up their tents and departed. I locked up for the night, so we won't be bothered."

He turned to the semi-conscious knife-man. "Well, Number Thirteen? Do you want to escape?"

The knife-man lifted his head. His little eyes were bright and keen with hatred, but he didn't speak.

Steve sighed. "He won't talk." He glanced from Murdoch to Kerrigan. "Well, you mopes, what have you got to say? Is it my show from now on, or isn't it?"

Murdoch sighed. "I guess it's all yours from here on, Shrimp. Number Thirteen is just your size. Neither Kerrigan nor I could pass for him."

Klaw bent over and tapped the knife-man on the shoulder.

"Take off your coat, pal. I have your hat right here."

The fellow obeyed sullenly, and Steve changed clothes with

him, transferring his two automatics to his new coat pockets. He put the felt hat on, and pulled the brim low over his eyes.

"How'm I doing?" he asked.

"I guess you'll pass in the dark," said Murdoch. "But wait till von Rieber sees you in the light!"

"I hope I see him first!" Steve said.

Kerrigan stood up. "All right, let's get started."

They tied up the three prisoners, and carried them down into the cellar, where they left them in the dark. On the way out, Murdoch used the phone to call the F.B.I. Field Office and ask them to come and get the three spies. Then they went out the back way.

"Give us two minutes, Shrimp," Murdoch said.

Klaw nodded.

They started away, and Kerrigan stopped and turned around. "Take care of yourself, Shrimp," he said. "You wouldn't look nice with a bullet in you."

"Or a knife," Murdoch added.

"Cheerful ghost!"

"So long, Shrimp," they said. "See you in hell!"

They hurried away.

Klaw waited two minutes, then he made his way along the rear, to the back of the photographer's shop. In the alley along-side the store, there was a small florist's truck. The lettering on the panel said, *Forrest Florists*. There was no address.

A man sat hunched behind the wheel. When he heard Steve he turned around.

"Who's that?" he demanded.

"Number Thirteen," said Steve.

"Get in. Hurry up. What kept you?"

Steve mumbled something, and climbed in the back of the truck.

"Close the doors, you fool!" said the driver.

Steve obeyed. He pulled the doors shut, leaving himself in pitch darkness. The truck started, and he felt it swerve as it pulled out of the alley into the street.

A grating in front opened, and the driver spoke through it. "Are they after you?"

"No."

"Did you kill him?"

"Right through the hat," said Steve.

The driver chuckled. "The same hat trick you used on the other one. Von Rieber will like it."

After that, the driver didn't try to make conversation, and Steve was just as glad.

They rode for about twenty minutes, then Steve felt the speed decrease. They slowed down and the front of the truck slanted downward. They must be descending a ramp.

At last they came to a halt. Steve went to open the back doors. His eyes became narrow, and his lips tightened to a thin line of resignation.

The doors were locked on the outside!

From beyond the doors, a voice spoke in gleeful triumph. "*Heil* Hitler! You American jackass! Did you think to fool me? You did not know, did you, that *Number Thirteen is a deaf mute!*"

"So that's why he wouldn't talk!" said Steve.

"Wait till I bring von Rieber!" the voice chuckled. "He will enjoy this!"

CHAPTER 5
DEATH IS NO JOKE

FIVE MINUTES later, Steve heard the voice of Major Carl Friedrich von Rieber. It was an authoritative voice, cold and measured.

"Which one of you is it in there? Which one of the Suicide Squad have we captured?"

"Number Thirteen," said Steve.

Von Rieber chuckled. "You may surrender if you wish. I would like to talk with you."

"When you open these doors," Steve told him, "I'm coming out shooting."

"In that case, my dear sir, we shall not open the doors at all, till you are dead. We will flood the interior of the truck with cyanide. It will be a much easier way to dispose of you."

"Don't look now," said Steve, "but there's a rat prowling around outside this truck."

"Ha, ha," said von Rieber. "You can joke even with death, eh? I admire you. But you will die in vain. Your ships will continue to go down."

"That's where you're wrong," said Steve. "I know what makes them explode."

"Indeed! Perhaps you will tell me?"

"Why yes. Your man Moynes does it. He goes across the

street with that camera of his, supposedly to get the pictures of the new men developed. Each time he goes, he has it filled with explosive. Everyone is searched before entering the plant, but the guard never thinks of searching that camera. That's how Moynes brings the explosive into the pier."

"Damn you!" exclaimed von Rieber. "You have guessed it! Who else knows this?"

"I just figured it out. I think best in the dark."

"Tell me *your* name, my friend. I would wish to know which of the Suicide Squad you are—before I finish you off."

"Tell me your name," Steve said, "and I'll tell you mine."

"What do you mean? My name is von Rieber!"

"Like hell it is! I met von Rieber once. I'd remember his voice anywhere. You're not von Rieber."

There was silence for a moment. Steve heard them shuffling about outside the truck, then he heard someone climb up into the cab in front.

Grimly he took the two automatics out of his pockets, and stepped close to the little peep-door in front of the truck. They were going to shoot the cyanide in now.

He waited tensely, until the door was yanked open. Then he thrust one of the automatics out through the opening, and blasted three shots quickly.

Some one screamed, and he heard a heavy body fall. He put his face close to the opening, and saw the body lying across the wheel, a small copper tank with a nozzle still clasped close in one arm. He recognized the face of the dead man—Braun, the photographer. This was the one who had driven him here.

31

He tried to peer further out, but he could not get a glimpse of von Rieber. He heard von Rieber's voice, raised in a shout:

"*Himmel!* He has killed Braun. Curt! Get up there! Get that tank. Feed him the cyanide!"

KLAW SMILED grimly. He waited a moment, till he saw a hand reaching up to pull down the body of Braun.

He fired once, and shattered the wrist. A man screamed again.

And suddenly he heard the sounds of shooting from somewhere else in the building. The shots were heavy, thunderous and reverberating with a smooth rhythm which he recognized. Nobody shot like that except the team of Kerrigan and Murdoch. They had followed the truck in the station wagon, and now they were fighting their way in.

Through the din of the gunfire, Steve could hear von Rieber's voice raised in a shout, but the words themselves were drowned in the roar of the two pair of thirty-eights.

Klaw stepped away from the opening. He didn't have to worry about that cyanide now. With Kerrigan and Murdoch in the building, these Nazis would be too busy to try to use the tank.

He moved over to the back doors, felt in the darkness for the location of the lock, and then stepped back two paces. He pointed his right-hand automatic at the spot where he thought the lock should be and emptied the last three shots into it. A crack of light appeared between the doors, and then they sagged open.

Stephen Klaw came out of that truck like a hurricane.

For a moment he was almost blinded by the light. But then he saw that he was in a sort of basement garage. Half a dozen of the

Nazis were near the truck, and they were firing up at a balcony where Kerrigan and Murdoch stood. They must have come in from up above rather than by the ramp, and had shot their way down here. On that balcony, overlooking the wide expanse of floor on which there were almost a dozen trucks and cars, there was a large portrait of the megalomaniac who called himself the Führer of the Germans. And Johnny Kerrigan, who must have picked up the knife with which Number Thirteen had tried to kill him, was shooting with one hand, while slashing the picture with the other.

Down below, the Nazis were returning the fire of Kerrigan and Murdoch, but at the same time they were uttering cries of anguish at each slash of Johnny's knife.

For just a moment Steve Klaw enjoyed the spectacle, then he joined the fight. His single automatic joined its sharp bark to the deep-throated roar of his two partners' guns, and the Nazis, taken by surprise in the flank, went down like sheep to the slaughter.

Three of them threw down their guns and raised their hands in token of surrender. The others were dead or disabled.

Kerrigan and Murdoch came down the steps to meet Klaw.

"Hi, mopes," said Steve. "Your guns certainly made sweet music for my ears. They were going to feed me cyanide."

"Just what you need for your disposition," Kerrigan said.

They kept the prisoners covered, and Kerrigan's eyes widened as he spotted a familiar figure among them.

"Savage!" he exclaimed. "Hugo Savage! So you're one of them!"

HUGO SAVAGE was indeed among the prisoners. But he exclaimed, "For God's sake, let me take my arms down. I'm not one of this crowd. They kidnaped me—"

"Ha, ha!" said Steve.

Savage looked at him. "What—what—why are you laughing?"

"How are you, *Herr* Major Carl Friedrich von Rieber?"

"No, no—"

"Listen, Shrimp," said Johnny Kerrigan. "Is this the guy that's supposed to be von Rieber?"

"It's the guy who claimed to be von Rieber," Steve said. "He talked to me while I was in the truck. I told him he wasn't von Rieber."

Hugo Savage, *alias* Major Carl Friedrich von Rieber, closed his eyes. "It is true," he muttered. "Von Rieber is dead. He committed suicide last year, when you three hellions checkmated him. But the Gestapo in Berlin was unwilling to give you the satisfaction of learning that he had committed suicide. So they ordered me to assume his name and continue his organization. I came to this country thirty years ago; I worked in the Secret Service of the Kaiser during the last war, and then I worked for the Third Reich. You see, men like Moynes and me were above suspicion, for we had been here so long. You could not understand that a nation might have planned for so far ahead, and planted its agents here. But never for a moment—in defeat or in victory—did we give up the shining plan for world conquest!"

"Do you think Germany will put it over this time?" said Dan.

"Perhaps. Perhaps not. But if not this time, then next time."

His voice became intense and passionate with fanatical fervor. "Mark my words, Germany will try and try, and try again—until one day she rules the entire world."

"Nice people," said Steve Klaw.

Hugo Savage's shoulders slumped. "But I—I have failed. You three have bested me, as you bested von Rieber before me. There is nothing left but death."

He faced them, his eyes pleading. Then he glanced toward the truck.

"Perhaps you will grant me this last favor? I fought you tooth and nail, yes. But you have won. Will you extend this favor to the vanquished? I do not like the thought of the hangman's noose."

Johnny and Dan and Steve exchanged swift glances.

Steve Klaw sighed. "All right," he said.

Hugo Savage nodded. He turned and walked slowly toward the truck, his feet dragging as if heavy with leaden weights.

And slowly he reached for the cyanide tank, put his hand on the valve, and the nozzle to his mouth.

Johnny Kerrigan shuddered. "Move over, Death," he said.

TARGETS FOR
THE FLAMING ARROW

CHAPTER 1
THE SUPREME PLAN

O N THE seventeenth of August, a furtive Rumanian walked into the United States Consulate in Berne, Switzerland, and whispered that he had information to sell.

Closeted with one of the attaches, he put on a mysterious air, and said that he could tell about the plans of the Flaming Arrow to wreck the United States war effort.

The attache frowned. "The Flaming Arrow? What are you talking about?"

The Rumanian became more mysterious, and at the same time more furtive and frightened.

"It is the name of the one who can win the war for the Axis. He has been in America now for three years. But only three men in all the world know who the Flaming Arrow really is. Those three are Hitler, Himmler, and Tojo, of Japan. The Axis has paid ten million dollars over to the account of the Flaming Arrow, and there are ninety millions more in banks in every neutral country which he can call upon. For that sum, the Flaming Arrow has agreed to destroy American war power completely."

"You're mad!" said the attache.

"Mad? You think perhaps that I dream this? Let me tell you:

They kept up a steady fire as the boosted
the boy through the window.

There is a school not far from Berlin, where the Nazis train the youngsters who are smuggled into America to enter the ranks of the Flaming Arrow!"

The little Rumanian became eager, almost voluble. "But that is not all. In Formosa, there is a small island, in the middle of a large lake. None dares go near that island, for it is under the special protection of the Emperor. On that island other men are trained—men of a strange, vicious mountain race. They are little, wiry men, taken from Korea as children, and dedicated to the service of the Flaming Arrow. These men, too, have been smuggled into America. All are ready for the day when the Supreme Plan of the Flaming Arrow is ready for execution. On that day the Flaming Arrow will wreck America!"

The attache was annoyed. "Look here, my man, you've been smoking opium—"

"But no! I swear to you that this is all true. I alone have stumbled upon the clue, and I will sell it to you. Cable your government. Ask them. They know of the Flaming Arrow. Ask them how much you may pay me for information that will save your country!"

"All right," the attache agreed reluctantly. "Come back tomorrow morning at ten o'clock."

So a cable in code went off to the State Department: *What do you know about Axis agent named Flaming Arrow? Am offered information in re above but believe it of no value. Are you interested?*

Then the attache promptly forgot all about it. But he was awakened at two o'clock in the morning by an urgent radio message in reply: *"Get all information possible. Urgent. Flaming Arrow greater menace than fifty divisions!"*

Thoroughly aroused, the attache dressed hurriedly and went to the address which the Rumanian had left with him.

He was five minutes too late. The squalid room in which the informer lived was a mass of flames. Firemen forced their way in, and came out bearing the body of the Rumanian. There was still a bit of flickering life left in him as they laid him in the street, with a two-foot arrow protruding from his chest.

The attache thought of the name of the Axis agent whom this informer had wished to betray: The Flaming Arrow!

The shaft of the arrow was metal, charred and blackened from end to end. The Rumanian's clothes were burned away from his body.

The Swiss fire chief exclaimed, "The arrow must have burst into flames when it struck him!"

And someone in the crowd whispered, "It is the mark of the Flaming Arrow!"

The word spread quickly. In a moment, the crowd had faded away. Even the firemen and police looked a bit fearful.

The attache was unaware of all this as he bent over the dying Rumanian, listening to the gurgle of sound which trickled from the informer's lips. Only a word or two was he able to distinguish;

"My brother... in America... find him...."

Then the man was dead.

NINE DAYS later, a man sat in an office on the sixth floor of the Scanda Building, in Stockholm, Sweden. There were papers on his desk, and half a dozen photographs, as well as a roll of developed film. The photographs were weird things, showing a group of small and wiry men, all attired in similar fashion, with short leather jerkins, and metal helmets. Their faces were Mongolian, with such small eyes that they might have belonged to some species of reptile. Their hands were encased in leather gloves, and on their backs they carried a long bow and a quiver of arrows.

One of the pictures showed a group of these men marching down to a ship. The picture had been taken at night, apparently with a flashlight bulb, and it was remarkably clear.

The man who sat at the desk with these photographs before him jiggled the hook of his telephone and barked impatiently, "You must put me through to America at once. I want Washington!"

"This is the transatlantic operator, sir.. Your connection is being completed. We will have Mr. Hedges in the State Department in a moment."

"Good—"

Whatever the stocky man might have been about to say, he never said it.

The arrow thrummed its deadly hum of doom, winging through the open window. It thudded into his chest, carrying him backward in his chair, crashing to the floor.

His frantic grip knocked the telephone with him. He lay on his back on the floor, his knees in the air, folded over the chair seat, and the arrow protruding almost three feet from his chest. His body twitched in the throes of death.

From the receiver came an impatient voice: "Bardo! I say there, Bardo! This is Hedges of the State Department!"

There was a jiggling sound, then Hedges's voice again: "Operator! There's nobody on here. What happened to that call?"

The dying Bardo's face became contorted with a strange and fearful effort as he struggled to bring his bloody lips close to the mouthpiece of the phone.

"Hedges!" he gasped. "Hedges, listen! This is Bardo...." He

was silent for a second, then his voice erupted once more in a weird and frightful gurgle. "The Flaming Arrow… got me. Look out for the little… bowmen. They're smuggling thousands of them… planning something big… for September first…."

It was then that a strange phenomenon occurred; the arrow which was quivering in his chest burst into bright and incandescent flame.

It was like the all-consuming fire of an incendiary bomb, unbearably hot, sizzlingly brilliant, hissing with the sound of burning magnesium. The flame raced down the shaft of the arrow, as if it had been greased with wax. In a moment, the man's body was completely enveloped by the flaming holocaust, which had already spread to the rug, licking out hungrily at the rest of the room….

CHAPTER 2
TRAP…?

"WHAT'S THIS I hear about a flaming arrow?" Stephen Klaw demanded, the moment he got into Dan Murdoch's room at the Berkshire Hotel.

Dan Murdoch was in shirt sleeves. The window was open, but he had the blind pulled all the way down. He was examining a charred stick of metal, about three feet long. There was an arrowhead point on it, and that, too, was blackened as if from a bath of fire.

Murdoch grinned, and exhibited the stick.

Klaw took it, and turned it around curiously in his hands. "A steel arrow!" he exclaimed. "Where did you get it?"

Murdoch chuckled. "It came to me out of the blue!"

"You mean someone shot at you?"

"Nothing else but!"

Klaw's eyes began to glitter. "I take it we're on a case?"

"You bet!" He picked up his coat from the bed, exhibited a rent in the left sleeve. "That's how close it came. It grazed me and hit a brick wall. The next second it burst into flames. There was a small magnesium pencil bomb fitted in the shaft. It burned like the devil for about thirty seconds, and that's all that's left!"

Stephen Klaw said thoughtfully, "If it had hit you, there'd be nothing left of you but blackened bones and a few teeth!"

They were interrupted by a knock at the door. The knock was immediately repeated, three times in quick succession, then three times slow.

"That'll be Johnny!" said Murdoch.

He went over and unlocked the door. Big, red-headed Johnny Kerrigan entered. "What's all this about?" he growled. "Why this hocus-pocus about meeting in secret, Dan, you registered here under a phony name—"

"Take it easy, Johnny," said Murdoch. "It's by order of the State Department. We're going after the Flaming Arrow!"

"Ah!" said Kerrigan. "Now you're talking! When do we start?"

"Don't get ants in your pants," said Murdoch. "We're waiting for the Chief. He's coming here with Under-secretary Hedges of the State Department. This is no pushover, guys. The Flaming Arrow is 'way over the class of anything we've ever handled. Take a look at this arrow, for instance. It was shot at me, less than an hour after I had talked with the Chief over long distance, and he had assigned me to the case."

Once more there was a knock at the door. This time Murdoch admitted the Director of the Federal Bureau of Investigation, accompanied by Under-secretary of State Hedges.

Hedges was nervous and jumpy. "You'll have to excuse me, boys," he said after he had been introduced. "I've been on edge for ten days. And so has everybody in Washington. Twice in the last ten days we've come within an ace of getting valuable information on the Flaming Arrow; and twice, it was snatched from under our noses by the Flaming Arrow's agents—once in Berne, and once in Stockholm. Yesterday, our most valuable man in Europe was killed by a flaming arrow before he could transmit details to us. The arrow that killed him burst into flames and destroyed everything in his room. The only new thing we learned from him was that the grand coup of the Flaming Arrow is planned for September first. This is the twenty-seventh. That gives us only four days."

HEDGES LOOKED at Murdoch, and the arrow in his hand. "As for you, there's nothing you can do. It's quite apparent that you are known to the Flaming Arrow. The fact that he made this attempt on your life is sufficient to impair your usefulness. As for you two—" he nodded to Kerrigan and Klaw—"I'm afraid that in asking you to undertake this job, I'm giving you a suicide assignment. But your Director here tells me that it's just such assignments you welcome." He permitted himself a faint smile. "I understand that you are known in the F.B.I. as the Suicide Squad."

Neither Kerrigan nor Murdoch nor Klaw made any reply. Though it was perfectly true that they were called the Suicide Squad, they took no special pride in it. Theirs was a devil-may-care philosophy of life, based on the theory that all three of them had long ago forfeited any right to expect to enjoy old age—ripe or otherwise.

Johnny Kerrigan had once punched a senator's son in the nose; Dan Murdoch had once shot a coupier to death in a crooked gambling joint; and Stephen Klaw had once told the chairman of a Senate investigation committee to go to hell when he had been asked why he had shot to kill in a fight with a band of gunmen.

Any other three federal agents would have been dismissed for these offenses. But the records of Kerrigan, Murdoch and Klaw were such that even a Senatorial indignation would not have stood against popular demand. The Chief of the F.B.I. had taken advantage of their records to effect a compromise. He had arranged for them to be placed on special duty, where they would never be in danger of coming in contact with anyone whose feelings were likely to be hurt.

From that time on, the Director had made it a practice to assign them to such cases as would ordinarily have demanded a call for volunteers.

Thus had been formed the Suicide Squad. Together with a couple of other wild and irreconcilable hellions, they had made a blazing swath of gunfire through the underworld. There had been five of them at the start; then only four; then three—Kerrigan and Murdoch and Klaw. Tomorrow there might be only two, or one—or none....

But one thing was certain: if the Suicide Squad was wiped out, it would not be without bloody cost to the party of the other part.

Now, here in this room in the Berkshire Hotel, they were being offered the kind of assignment they lived for; and they were eager to get their teeth into it. Especially since the arrow had been launched at Murdoch.

"Let's get down to cases, Mr. Hedges," Stephen Klaw said impatiently. "If there's only a matter of four days between us and the end of the country, let's not waste any more time talking!"

Under-secretary Hedges nodded. "All right," he said curtly, "I'll give it to you straight. The United States Government wants the Flaming Arrow within four days. We don't know who he is, and we don't know his plan for September first. But we do know that the Flaming Arrow is responsible for the three disasters which occurred on the same day last month—one in Oregon, one in Texas and one in Maryland."

Hedges paused, looking from one to the other of them. "And we are further convinced that those three pieces of sabotage were just rehearsals for the big coup four days from now."

"So all you want us to do," Johnny Kerrigan said, "is to lay this Flaming Arrow by the heels—without knowing who or what he is!"

HEDGES SPREAD his hands helplessly. "I can't tell you very much more, I confess. We have learned only fragments.

TARGETS FOR THE FLAMING ARROW

We know that the Flaming Arrow is smuggling two groups into this country for his big show. One of those groups consists of specially trained Nazi youths; the other group consists of a wild and savage tribe of men recruited by the Japs in Korea, and raised on a secret island in Formosa, where they have been educated for years, solely for the purpose of enrollment with the Flaming Arrow. The ramifications of the Flaming Arrow's spy organization must go pretty deep, for he was able to learn apparently, that you, Murdoch, had been assigned to the case. So there is every reason to believe that you three men will be walking to your deaths. Yet I must ask you to dig around, to use your connections in the underworld, to use anything and everything that may come to your hand, in one supreme effort to smoke out the Flaming Arrow within four days—"

Hedges was interrupted by the quick, sharp ring of the telephone on the night table.

Dan Murdoch frowned. "It may be for you, sir," he said to the Director of the F.B.I. "Nobody knows that I'm here—"

The Director shook his head. "Nobody knows Hedges and I are here, either. We didn't tell a soul where we were going!"

Murdoch shrugged, and picked up the phone. "Yes?"

The voice at the other end was that of a woman.

"Please don't ask any questions, and don't waste time," the woman said hurriedly. "Listen to me closely if you want to save your country."

"Go on!" Murdoch said, suddenly tense. He had caught the note of urgency in her voice.

"I dare not take the time to explain anything now. But if

you want to pick up some information about that certain party whose arrow you have, then be at the Dardanelles Restaurant tonight at six sharp. Come alone. Promise?"

"I promise," said Dan Murdoch solemnly.

"I accept your word. If you break it, you will only bring death to yourself as well as to me. Goodbye!"

There was a tight smile on Murdoch's dark and handsome face as he laid the receiver gently down in its cradle.

"A break!" he whispered. "An unexpected break!"

Swiftly, he told them what the woman had said.

"You lucky stiff!" Kerrigan exclaimed.

But Under-secretary Hedges was not so enthusiastic. "It may be a trap, Murdoch!" he warned. "In fact, it *must* be a trap. Don't you see? The Flaming Arrow tried for you once and failed. Now he's using this woman to lure you to your death!"

"I certainly hope so!" Murdoch said fervently.

Hedges threw up his hands in disgust. "What kind of men are you three?" He turned appealingly to the Director of the F.B.I. "Look here, you've got to forbid Murdoch to go there. Do you understand? Tell him now that he's not to go near the Dardanelles Restaurant!"

The Director smiled grimly. "Sorry Hedges. You've given them their assignment. I've given them *carte blanche*. I make it a rule never to interfere with the Suicide Squad once they've started on a job. It's like trying to take a bone away from a bulldog!"

CHAPTER 3
INTERNATIONAL ALLIANCE

A T SIX o'clock sharp Dan Murdoch entered a greasy, foul-smelling Turkish restaurant on Allen Street, down on the lower East Side.

The sign outside read:

DARDANELLES RESTAURANT
Native Turkish Cooking
C. Foolhabi, Prop.

The proprietor was a short, moon-faced man with a pair of thick black eyebrows, and a heavy, drooping mustache. He got up from a table where he was playing checkers, bowed to Murdoch, and conducted him wordlessly to a table.

There were four or five checker games going on among the customers at the various tables, and each game had one or two kibitzers. A radio was playing somewhere in the rear, and a waitress was clattering dishes, and discussions were going on in several languages at some of the other tables.

The whole atmosphere was noisy and unrestful, not in the least adapted to a quiet game of checkers.

Almost every one in the place was drinking thick black Turkish coffee, without cream, and a few of them were eating sandwiches.

The proprietor didn't waste any time on Murdoch. He dropped a greasy menu in front of him, and went back to his checker game.

Murdoch looked around for the woman who had phoned him. There were half a dozen women in the busy place, and any one of them might have been the one he sought. She hadn't given him any clue to her appearance. He could only sit and wait for her to make herself known to him.

He had so maneuvered to get a chair against the wall. He could see all of the restaurant, and at least no one here would be able to put a knife in his back without his seeing it first. Of course, an arrow might be launched from the kitchen, or a gun might be fired from there. But he had to chance that.

When the waitress came over to him, he ordered coffee. He had been watching her serve several of the other customers, and he was trying to guess how she fitted into this place, among these swarthy, dark-complexioned people. For she was distinctly a northern type, tall and fair-skinned, with golden-yellow hair braided high on her head, and clear blue eyes. Dan Murdoch got a distinct shock when he glimpsed the tautness of her lips, the tinge of fright in her eyes.

"Yes, sir," she said. "Coffee. Anything else?"

Murdoch stiffened as he recognized the voice. She was the one who had spoken to him over the phone.

He gave no sign of recognition. He merely said, "That's all."

She bent over the table, wiping an imaginary spot, and she spoke very low. "You kept your word? You came alone?"

"Yes."

"That's good. Watch the man with the wart on the side of his nose—the one who is playing checkers with the man with the thin hands. The man with the wart is the one you are to follow,

52

but the one with the thin hands is the dangerous one. He can move like a magician, and before you know it there is a knife in your throat!"

Murdoch wanted to ask her a question, but she turned and hurried away.

He let his gaze stray to the table where the two men were playing checkers. The one with the wart on the side of his nose was a stocky, swarthy-skinned fellow, with a shock of black unkempt hair that came down over his eyes. He had thick, sensual lips, and a bull-like neck. He looked like a cutthroat from the waterside of any one of a dozen European cities.

It seemed incongruous that he should be playing checkers with the man with the thin hands. That one was an ascetic man, whose age was difficult to determine. He was carefully dressed in black, with a white shirt and a black tie. His hands were thin and long.

THE WAITRESS came back with a cup of the thick, black coffee, and placed it before Murdoch. As she bent over him, her lips moved: "The man with the wart is Dagomar. It is he who guides the Flaming Arrow's recruits into shore at night. The other one is Gallieni, whose duties I do not know. Finish your coffee quickly and go out and wait. Dagomar leaves every night at seven o'clock. Follow him and you will find where the recruits land."

"Who are you?" Murdoch demanded. "Why are you doing this?"

She smiled faintly. "Don't forget to drink your coffee," she whispered. "It would look suspicious if you left without drinking it. They know who you are. If they thought I was helping you, they would kill me."

She wrote out a check for the coffee, and hurried away to attend to other customers.

Murdoch sat for a moment, looking down into the thick, muddy liquid. She had urged him to drink it. He had no way of knowing, at this moment, whether she was a friend or a foe. Under-secretary Hedges had been convinced that this was a trap. It wouldn't have been difficult for her to slip a lethal dose of poison into the coffee.

Murdoch raised his eyes, and saw that Gallieni, the man with the thin hands, was watching him. Gallieni swiftly shifted his glance back to the checker-board, and said something to Dago-mar. But the man with the wart on his nose did not turn.

Murdoch shrugged. It was easy enough to find out if his coffee was poisoned. All he had to do was drink it.

He raised the cup to his lips. His hand was steady.

Just then someone screamed, back in the kitchen.

It was a dreadful scream, fraught with mortal terror and pain, stiffening the patrons in their chairs as if they had been shocked by a high-voltage current.

Murdoch was on his feet in a split-second. A single glance told him that the blonde waitress was not out here. She must be in the kitchen.

Foolhabi, the proprietor, sat frozen in his seat, his mouth open and his eyes wide. Gallieni had stopped in the act of making a move. Dagomar was half-crouched in his chair, as if ready to spring out of it.

But it was Dan Murdoch who reached the kitchen first, with his revolver in his hand.

It was the blonde waitress who had screamed. She was lying on the floor, on her back, with a long, feathered arrow quivering in her shoulder. The Turkish cook stood in a far corner, blubbering with terror. As Murdoch entered he pointed with a shaking hand to the open back door, indicating the direction from which the arrow had come.

Murdoch dropped to his feet beside the waitress, but just as he did so the arrow burst into bright, fierce flame that drove him back by its very fierceness.

Murdoch saw the fire had started in the feathered part of the arrow. It raced down the length of the shaft, licking at the waitress's dress.

Murdoch's face was grim. He reached out and seized the shaft. It seared skin and hand unmercifully, but he yanked hard, tearing the arrow out of the wound. It came easily, for the tip was not deeply embedded. The wound wasn't fatal, but the fire would have finished what the arrow had begun.

Dan flung the arrow through the open door, into the back yard, where it burned itself out on the concrete.

In that moment of bright light, Murdoch caught a glimpse of two small, wiry figures, so strange and horrid that it was almost incredible. They were like some savage beings from another planet, moving in long and sinuous strides that were altogether out of proportion to their small bodies. They were both clad exactly alike, in some kind of leather jerkins, and their heads were tightly encased in metal helmets. Beneath the helmets their yellowish faces gleamed evilly.

EACH OF those small but monstrous figures had a long bow in his hand, and a quiver on his back. In the moment that Murdoch glimpsed them, they were fitting arrows into the bows. Then the light went out, and the yard outside was plunged in darkness. But the kitchen was brightly illuminated, and Murdoch knew that the bowmen of the Flaming Arrow were intent upon finishing their job.

He threw himself flat on the floor. His right hand throbbed unmercifully with the pain of the burn, but he carried two guns, and—like the other members of the Suicide Squad—he was proficient with both hands. He drew his right-hand gun with his left hand, and sent a fast barrage out into the night.

He had the satisfaction of hearing one scream, pitched high above the blast of the gunfire. But the second of the two must have gone unscathed, for a moment later an arrow hummed through the air and bit into the floor, barely an inch from where he lay.

Murdoch sprang to his feet and raced out into the yard. His right hand hung useless, but he had his other gun out. For a moment, when he emerged into the night, he could see nothing. But he kept running blindly, and almost tripped over the body of one of the Korean bowmen. He recovered his balance, but it was that near-fall which saved him, for a second arrow whined past him and buried itself in the framework of the building. The arrow in the kitchen had already burst into flames, and the cook and several others were fighting the spreading fire. Murdoch paid no attention to that. He had spotted the second bowman, over near a corner of the yard, crouching, fitting a third arrow to his bow.

Grimly, Murdoch threw down his gun and pulled the trigger. The Korean uttered a high-pitched screech, and fell forward on top of his bow and arrow.

The arrow burst into fire, and the leather-jerkined killer's body was enveloped in a sheet of flame.

A police whistle was shrilling somewhere out in the street. Someone was screaming for the fire engines. A single glance told Murdoch that the fire in the kitchen was beyond control. He rushed back, remembering the waitress, but the kitchen was deserted. She must either have been carried out by the cook, or else she had recovered consciousness and had made her way out alone.

Murdoch swung away, and raced to the alley at the side of the yard. The agony of his seared hand was becoming almost unbearable. He ran out into the street, emerging at the mouth of the alley just in time to see the mob of patrons emerging from the restaurant. Among them he glimpsed the blonde waitress, leaning on the arm of Foolhabi, the frightened proprietor.

He gave her only a single glance, then he searched for Dagomar and Gallieni. He spotted them on the fringe of the crowd, whispering hurriedly. Then they separated, Gallieni going east, and Dagomar west, past the dark mouth of the alley where Murdoch stood.

Murdoch stepped out in Dagomar's wake, followed him for half a dozen paces, then saw the slim, wiry figure of Stephen

Klaw directly across the street. Farther up the block he spotted the big, powerful form of Johnny Kerrigan.

They were both running swiftly toward the fire, and Murdoch smiled. True to his promise, he had gone alone to the Darda-nelles Restaurant. But there was nothing in his agreement to prevent Kerrigan and Klaw from covering the outside, and they had done just that, remained about a block away.

WITH A quick lift of his good hand, he indicated the figure of the hurrying Dagomar. Stephen Klaw got the signal, and nodded. It was all he needed. These three men had worked together for so long, that they knew each other's thoughts and intentions almost subconsciously. Anyone else might have wondered just what Murdoch wanted done about Dagomar—whether he wanted him stopped, or followed. But Stephen Klaw knew very well that if Murdoch had wanted to stop the man, he'd have done it himself. Therefore, he wanted him followed.

Klaw turned and signalled to Kerrigan, who swiftly turned and hurried back to the car which he had left parked. Klaw waved to Murdoch, and headed back in the direction he had been going, keeping abreast of Dagomar, on the other side of the street.

Murdoch waited only another moment, to make sure that Klaw and Kerrigan were on the trail. Then he made his way through the crowd in front of the restaurant to the ambulance which had come clanging to the scene with the fire engines.

"Fix this hand, will you?" he said to the ambulance attendant. His face was white with pain.

Due to the shortage of doctors, there was only an attendant

on the ambulance instead of the usual interne, but the young fellow was competent, and did a good job on the burned hand, using tannic acid.

"Boy," he said, "you sure got it good."

"I say he got it goot!" said a hearty voice at his elbow.

Murdoch turned, and saw the stout, round-faced proprietor of the burning restaurant.

Dan's eyes narrowed. "Where's that waitress?"

Foolhabi spread his hands helplessly. "She gone fast. After doctor fix her oop, she scr-ram."

Murdoch glanced at the ambulance attendant. "Was the wound serious?"

"No. Only a flesh wound."

"You haff save her!" Foolhabi exclaimed, patting Murdoch on the back. " I haff see you pool out dose burning arrow. If not for you—*poof*—she is only ashes!"

"But where did she go?"

Foolhabi shrugged his shoulders. "Whom could tell—"

He was interrupted by an angry, anxious voice. "Where's my niece? What's happened to Hildegarde? Where is she?"

They saw a tall, stoop-shouldered gentleman, with a pair of spectacles sitting perilously low on his nose, who had pushed his way through the crowd.

Foolhabi uttered a groan. "Dose iss the oncle off the waitress. Professor Swenson. He comes effery night to taking her home."

The elderly professor pushed through to the ambulance, saw Foolhabi, and collared him.

"What have you done with my niece?" He gestured toward

the raging inferno which the restaurant had become. "Is she safe?"

"Yess, yess, Professor!" Foolhabi exclaimed. "She iss safe. She was shot by a flaming arrow, but this gentleman haff saved her. I haff seen with my own eyes how he haff pulled the burning arrow out. But for him she would be dead."

"Yes, yes," exclaimed the impatient professor. "But where is she now?"

Foolhabi shrugged. "While I do not look, she haff went away. Per'aps home, eh?"

Professor Swenson drew a deep breath, half of relief, half of doubt. He looked at Murdoch. "I'm sorry, sir. I should thank you for saving Hildegarde's life. But— but I'm so nervous these days. Please accept my expression of deepest gratitude. If there is ever anything I can do for you—I am Professor Ernst Swenson, Professor of Applied Chemistry at Corbin University."

"Glad to know you, sir," Dan said. "I'm Daniel Murdoch. I'd like to talk to you about your niece."

"It will be a pleasure. Will you come home with me? Hildegarde is no doubt home by this time—I hope!"

MURDOCH STAYED a few minutes longer to talk to the police. He showed them his F.B.I. identification, but didn't tell them what had brought him here. He merely said he had been having coffee in the restaurant when the leather-jerkined bowmen had attacked. He watched the charred remains of the one Korean, and the dead body of the other being removed in the morgue wagon, and he promised the police captain in charge to be down at headquarters later that evening. Then he went with Professor Swenson.

They took a cab uptown. On the way Professor Swenson told Murdoch how worried he had been of late about Hildegarde.

"I'm sure she's been mixing in some kind of dangerous business where a girl like her doesn't belong. Naturally, she feels she must do something to help the country. We came here as refugees from the Nazi tyranny, escaping with barely our lives. Hildegarde's mother and father died in the terror of 1933, and she has only me and her young brother, who is crippled. I manage to support them on my small salary as professor, but I am developing certain war inventions which should be of great service. I keep telling Hildegarde that she should not expose herself to danger, but she does not listen. For instance, she has taken the job as waitress in the Dardanelles Restaurant, in order to spy upon a certain Axis agent—the Flaming Arrow. This is too dangerous work for a girl. You see what happened tonight...."

They had reached Corbin University, and Professor Swenson led Murdoch across the campus to Carlyle Hall, where he lived.

"I have my laboratory and study here, and I lecture in the chemistry building across the way. It is very convenient."

He led the way down the corridor of Carlyle Hall, and stopped before Apartment Nine. "These are my quarters." He peered at Murdoch over his glasses and said, "You know, I have an idea that you are more than you seem. You were not there in the Dardanelles by accident, eh?"

Murdoch smiled. "Well, no."

Swenson got his door open, and stood aside for Murdoch to enter.

Murdoch stepped inside, and at once knew that he was in a trap. Half a dozen little yellow men, clad in leather jerkins and helmets, swarmed over him, pinning his one good arm to his side, wrapping their octopus-like arms around him.

"Indeed, my dear Murdoch," Professor Swenson said ironically, "it is a pleasure to entertain you here!" He had taken off his glasses, and now his eyes shone malevolently, with a fiercely burning flame of hatred. "Your search for the Flaming Arrow is over, Murdoch! *I* am the Flaming Arrow!"

Murdoch stood helpless in the grip of the wiry little Koreans. He glanced across the room, and saw Hildegarde, the blonde waitress, sitting tensely upright in a chair, her hands in her lap, her face wracked by fear and anxiety. Her clothes were torn, but she sat erect, not daring to move, for one of the little brown Koreans was standing directly behind her, holding a keen-bladed knife near her throat.

Murdoch's gaze swung back to the elderly, stoop-shouldered figure of Professor Ernst Swenson.

"So you're the Flaming Arrow," he said. "You're the fabulous guy who's going to wreck America's war power on September first!"

Swenson was watching him with bright eyes. "Quite so, Murdoch. I see you have learned a good deal about my plans. Perhaps you can tell me how much more you have learned? You went to the Dardanelles Restaurant to meet my niece, didn't you?"

"Of course not," Murdoch lied gallantly. "I went there for a cup of Turkish coffee."

"You must excuse me for doubting you," Swenson said with a twisted smile. "At a time like this, with the fate of your country dependent upon your checkmating me, you'd hardly have gone looking for Turkish coffee."

"That's the way I am," Murdoch told him. "Whenever things get tense, I need Turkish coffee."

SWENSON SNAPPED his fingers impatiently. "Let's be done with pretense. You're going to talk, Murdoch. I want to know where those two partners of yours are. I'm sure that my niece, here, betrayed me to you in some manner. I don't know exactly how. She swears she didn't, and I hesitate to use drastic measures with her, for I still need her services—"

"Don't tell me she's working for you?"

"She is, indeed, Murdoch—"

Hildegarde Swenson burst out passionately, "He forces me to do it, Mr. Murdoch. If it weren't for my little brother—" She gasped and lapsed into silence as the little brown Korean, at a signal from Swenson, brought his knife closer to her throat.

"Quiet, my dear," said Swenson. He turned back to Murdoch. "One of my Koreans shot her with a flaming arrow. The man is dead, so I can't question him. I don't know whether it was a mistake, or whether he detected her in an act of treachery. But it doesn't matter. *You*, my dear Murdoch, are going to talk. You are going to tell me just where your two partners are at this moment, and what they are doing!"

Murdoch smiled serenely. "Go to hell!"

Swenson's eyes flickered. He issued an order in a strange, weird tongue, and the little brown men leaped to obey. They dragged Murdoch across the room, into the laboratory beyond. Here, among test tubes and retorts, there was a trap-door in the floor. It was open, and one of the Koreans descended a few rungs of the ladder which led down into the dark cavern below.

It took five of them to handle Murdoch, even with his one hand useless. But they managed to get him down the ladder, partly by throwing him down the last half-dozen rungs. As Murdoch hit the cement floor below, he heard Swenson calling down to him softly, "Very soon, you shall be ready to talk freely. For the time being, I must leave you in the care of my Koreans."

The last thing Murdoch heard before the soundproof trap-door slammed shut above him was the girl's hysterical cry.

"You beast!" she was screaming at her uncle.

One of the Koreans snapped on an electric torch, and they pushed and dragged Murdoch over to a barred cell. He saw now that there were half a dozen such cells down here, and that one other was occupied by a boy of about thirteen. The child looked sick and emaciated in the quick glimpse that Murdoch got of him before his cell door clanged shut and the flashlight went out.

The Koreans moved about in the darkness outside the cell, apparently quite at home in the absence of light.

Murdoch called softly, "What do you say, sonny? How you doing?"

For a moment there was silence, then the thin voice of the boy, "Who—who are you?"

"Dan Murdoch, Special Agent of the Federal Bureau of Investigation."

"Did uncle get you, too?"

"Looks like it, sonny," Murdoch chuckled. "What the devil's he keeping you in here for?"

"He makes Hildegarde—my sister—do his dirty work for him. He tells her that if she won't do what he says, he'll beat me to death. He's got this whole place wired with explosive, and she knows if she ever sent the F.B.I. here, uncle would make the whole place blow up, with me in it. So she doesn't dare refuse to do what he asks."

"I see," Murdoch said softly. "What's your name, sonny?"

"Holgar."

"Holgar, eh? That's a noble name. Norwegian?"

"That's right," the boy said eagerly. "We're Norwegian, Hildegarde and I. And Swenson isn't really our uncle. My real name is Holgar Thornwald. Our father and mother were killed when Norway was invaded. Swenson—he's the Flaming Arrow— came in with the invading army, and Hildegarde and I were captured. At first Swenson was going to have us killed, then he decided to take us to America. He said we'd make a good front for him."

"How come you speak such good English?"

"Our mother was American!" Holgar said proudly.

CHAPTER 4
BEACH PARTY

IT WAS fortunate that Kerrigan and Klaw had a car with them when they undertook the job of tailing Dagomar, for he rounded the corner and got into a sedan which was waiting there.

Kerrigan kept on the tail of that sedan, winding a tortuous way through the crowded east side streets, then up the East River Drive, and across the Queensboro Bridge into Long Island.

Under the new dimout regulations, speed within the city boundaries was limited to twenty miles an hour, and their quarry apparently had no desire to become entangled with local law, for they adhered closely to that limit.

Johnny Kerrigan kept a half block behind them all the time, skillfully holding the sedan in sight.

"Dan must have had a nice time back there in the Dardanelles Restaurant," Kerrigan said gloomily. "Did you hear the shooting? Those were his guns. And what a fire!"

"I think Dan was hurt," Steve Klaw said. "He was holding his right hand away from him, high up. But I don't think it could have been bad."

The sedan ahead increased its speed as they hit out into the open country, heading toward the south shore.

"Hey!" said Kerrigan. "This gets interesting. Wonder who we're tailing."

Klaw shrugged. "I hope it's the Flaming Arrow."

They swung into the Merrick Road, and here the traffic regulations were even more stringent than in the city, for this was close to the coast line, and headlights were dangerous. Cars were scarce. Reflector signs at frequent intervals announced that only shielded parking lights might be used, and that speed must not exceed twelve miles an hour. Any motorist who was able to do so chose some other road, and as a result, the two G-men and their quarry had the highway almost entirely to themselves. Kerrigan doused his lights entirely....

The speedometer showed that they had covered almost sixty miles.

Klaw said, "I wonder where those birds get the gas. Honest citizens couldn't make a trip like this."

"They'll make one trip too many!" Johnny grumbled. "It begins to look as if Dan really put us on to something good. Those eggs look like they're heading for monkey business. There they go—turning off on that side road! I know this country like a book. That road leads down to the Mullhaven Estate!"

Stephen Klaw's eyes glittered. "Mullhaven! That's the guy who took a trip around the world in his private yacht in 1936, and got a medal from Hitler! He never gave the medal back, either!"

Kerrigan swung the car off the road, and parked it in a little culvert.

"We'll take it on foot from here!" he said.

The sedan ahead had turned off into the side road, and its tail lights had disappeared. Kerrigan and Klaw stalked it, moving cautiously down the side road.

Up ahead, they saw the lights of the Mullhaven estate, and

they were so close to the sea that they could hear the roar of"
the breakers. The Mullhaven house stood on a slight rise, and
from where Kerrigan and Klaw were they could see it clearly
through the trees; but they did not see the car which they had
been following. It had not pulled up to the house.

They stopped for a moment, perplexed, and then Klaw tugged
silently at Kerrigan's sleeve. He pointed in the opposite direction, down near the shore.

The car was there, close to the beach, parked without lights.
They were just able to discern its bulk, and the figures of three
or four men moving about it. There had been only two men in
the car they had followed, which meant that other men had been
down there on the beach to meet them.

AS THEY watched, they heard a slight sound and turned to
see the doors of the garage behind the Mullhaven house opening. A moment later, a station wagon drove out, with no lights
showing.

Kerrigan and Klaw pulled back into the shadows of a maple
tree, thinking that the station wagon would come down the
road toward the highway. But instead, it turned toward the
beach, and pulled up alongside the other car. Shadowy figures
moved around the two vehicles, and Kerrigan and Klaw were
able to discern the shapes of sub-machine guns under the arms
of several of them.

Silently, Johnny and Steve moved down toward the beach.
But they had hardly taken half a dozen steps when Klaw tapped
Kerrigan warningly on the shoulder. They both stopped.

Ten paces away, a sentry was standing guard at the side of the road, almost invisible except for the gleam of the metal barrel of the sub-machine gun which was cradled under his arm. He was facing the beach, with his back partly turned to Johnny and Steve. Apparently he was quite sure that he would hear any one approaching along the road.

Steve looked at Johnny, and tapped his own chest with his thumb, and Johnny nodded reluctantly. Immediately, Steve dropped down on all fours, and inched his way alone into the heavy underbrush.

A minute passed, and then a second and a third, while Johnny kept his eye on the sentry. The fellow was small and compactly built. He wore the same leather jerkin and helmet as those two bowmen who Dan Murdoch had killed at the Dardanelles. Slung across his back was a bow and a quiver of long arrows, as well as the sub-machine gun.

Suddenly, there was a slight noise in the underbrush, several feet behind the sentry. Kerrigan frowned. Steve must have stepped on a dry twig.

The sentry swung around, instantly alert. His gun pushed forward, finger on the trip, his eyes peering intently toward the spot whence the noise had come.

Johnny Kerrigan frowned. While the I man was alert like that, Steve wouldn't have a chance.

Swiftly, Johnny bent and picked up a pebble, flipped it with his thumb. The pebble skimmed through the air and landed in the middle of the road, a couple of feet behind the sentry, with a little crunching sound. The fellow spun around, shifting his gun, and in that moment Stephen Klaw leaped at him from out the underbrush. Steve hit him with a flying jump, and threw one arm forward, then swung sideways with it so that the heel of his thumb struck the fellow in the side of the neck. At the same time, Steve drove his left fist into the small of his back.

The fellow uttered a gurgling grunt as the neck blow partly paralyzed him, at the same time that the blow in the back threw him off balance. In that instant, Klaw threw his right arm around his throat and yanked him backward, driving the toe of his right shoe into the back of the fellow's knees. The man came tumbling backward, his arms flailing the air, and Steve put his left hand, with a handkerchief in it, into the sentry's open mouth.

Johnny Kerrigan jumped in and clamped a big hand around the fellow's trigger finger, preventing him from shooting off the sub-machine gun and warning his companions down on the beach.

A moment later they had the jerkined sentry efficiently gagged and bound.

They left him there, and Johnny picked up the sub-machine gun, while Steve took the bow and the quiver of arrows. Shoulder to shoulder they followed the road down to the beach.

THEY HALTED where the underbrush ceased, perhaps twenty yards from the station wagon and the car. They saw now that the armed men with submachine guns were leather-jerkined and helmeted like the sentry they had surprised. The only white men were the two they had followed in the sedan, and a third who had driven the station wagon down from the garage. This one was speaking heatedly to the one whom they had followed.

"I tell you, Dagomar," he was saying, "we can't afford to take another batch in tonight. There are still fourteen men from the last batch who have yet to report to the Flaming Arrow. If we take another bunch in tonight, and leave them loose in the city, they may be captured. It's better to postpone it. Signal the sub to come back tomorrow."

Dagomar grunted unwilling assent. "All right, Mullhaven. But I don't think the Flaming Arrow will like it. He'll want every man set and ready for September first, and if we wait till tomorrow with this last batch, it'll only give him three days to issue instructions to them."

"Nevertheless," Mullhaven said smoothly, "I think it should be done this way. It's too bad neither of us knows where to contact the Flaming Arrow, but since we don't, it's up to us to use our best judgment."

"Well, maybe you're right," said Dagomar. "In view of the fact that the damned Suicide Squad has been assigned to us, we better be careful. Those rumors about them must be true, all right."

"What do you mean? What rumors?"

"The rumors that they have charmed lives. Twice now we tried to get one of them—that Murdoch, the tall, handsome one. Twice the arrows missed him. And I think he killed two of the Koreans tonight."

Mullhaven cursed in a low, intense voice. "That damned Suicide Squad! We must get rid of them somehow. I wrote that in my last memo to the Flaming Arrow, but he told me to mind my own business. I hope he knows what he is doing."

"Don't worry about the Suicide Squad," said Dagomar. "The Flaming Arrow will take care of them. He knows one of them already, and as soon as we find out what the other two look like, we'll get them all—charmed lives or not!"

"Well," said Mullhaven, "let's not waste time. Signal the submarine, and get through with it."

"Okay. One arrow means come back at the same time tomorrow night, doesn't it?"

"Right," said Mullhaven. "And two arrows means come right in, the coast is clear."

Dagomar turned to one of the Korean bowmen and spoke to him swiftly in that queer, staccato tongue of theirs.

The Korean fitted an arrow to his bow, aimed it toward the sky and let fly.

The arrow winged high in the night, becoming almost lost to sight. Then suddenly it took fire, high in the air, and formed a brilliant, flaming arc out over the ocean.

Johnny Kerrigan and Stephen Klaw, crouching in the underbrush, glanced at each other.

"One arrow means come back tomorrow," Johnny repeated softly. "Two arrows means come on in, the coast is clear!"

A slow smile spread on the faces of each of them.

"Go to it, Shrimp," said Johnny. "If it works, it's a honey. You do your end, and I'll do mine!"

"Here goes!" said Stephen Klaw.

HE TOOK an arrow out of the quiver he had captured from the sentry, and swiftly fitted it to the bow. He got to his feet, and drew the arrow far back. Then he released the shaft, sent it swinging high up into the night.

The twang of the bow was loud and startling in the darkness. And the next moment the arrow burst into fire in the sky, and arced down into the sea.

Almost immediately, a bable of angry and excited voices broke out from the men around the station wagon.

"Who did that?" Mullhaven demanded angrily. "It was one of your damned Koreans, Dagomar! What the hell are we going to do about it?"

Dagomar faced toward the spot from which Klaw had shot the arrow, and a spew of strange words in that foreign tongue burst from his lips. He evidently thought that one of his Koreans had fired the arrow, and was bawling him out in his native language.

In the moment of surprise which the second arrow had caused, Johnny Kerrigan slipped away in the darkness, leaving Klaw alone. Steve stepped out from his place of concealment in the underbrush, carrying the bow and arrow ostentatiously in one hand. In his other hand he gripped one of his automatics, holding it behind him, hidden from the view of Dagomar and the others.

"I wish you'd talk to me in English," he said.

They all stared at him, open-mouthed, as if he were an apparition.

Steve stood there very quietly, grinning. He did not move even when Mullhaven clicked on a flashlight and turned it full on him.

"Who the devil are you?" Mullhaven demanded. The man's surprise had given way to anger now.

"Stephen Klaw, Special Agent of the Federal Bureau of Investigation, at your service," Klaw said.

"Klaw!" exclaimed Dagomar. "One of the Suicide Squad!"

"Pardon me for intruding," Steve said politely. "But you gentlemen are all under arrest!"

"Arrest!" Dagomar shouted. "There are ten of us here. Are you trying to commit suicide?"

"Ten of you?" Klaw said. "You'd better surrender. Put down your guns and raise your hands in the air!"

"You're mad!" Mullhaven exclaimed, keeping the flashlight centered on Steve's face. "How did you get past our sentry? There can't be anybody else with you—"

"Only the Army, the Navy, and the Marines," Klaw told him. Out of the corner of his eye he saw Johnny Kerrigan climb up into the station wagon, and get behind the wheel. He grinned, and brought the automatic out from behind his back. He fired practically from the hip, straight into the blinding cone of Mullhaven's flashlight.

The light disintegrated, to the accompaniment of a cry of anguish from Mullhaven. And at the same time, Kerrigan snapped on the bright headlights of the station wagon, flooding the beach with light, and silhouetting the group of men.

Dagomar uttered a curse, and then shouted a swift, vicious order in that foreign tongue to his Korean bowmen. They crouched low, raising their sub-machine guns as they swung toward the station wagon.

But they were blinded by the powerful headlights, and could see nothing. Dagomar lifted a revolver, with the intention of shooting out the headlights, but Stephen Klaw snapped a single shot at him, smashing his wrist. Then Johnny Kerrigan swung out on the running-board of the station wagon and sent one burst from his sub-machine gun ploughing into the sand at the feet of the massed Koreans.

Klaw threw away the bow and arrows, and came in charging at them like a halfback taking the ball through the line. He rammed viciously into one of the Koreans, sent the man sprawling, and snatched up the fellow's sub-machine gun. Gripping the weapon, he kept going right through the crowd until he emerged on the other side, clear of them.

KERRIGAN HAD held his fire after the first burst, and now one or two of the Koreans began pulling the trips of their quick-firers. They smashed one of the headlights, but by that time Kerrigan and Klaw had opened up with their sub-machine guns, Kerrigan giving it to them from in front, and Klaw taking them in the flank. They sent two bursts into the Koreans, cutting down almost half of them, and then suddenly the remainder of the bowmen threw down their guns in panic and raised their hands in the air. The spirit was knocked out of them by the sight of their leaders, Dagomar and Mullhaven, lying dead on the ground, together with half their companions.

Kerrigan and Klaw rounded them all up, then herded them up to the house on the hill, making them carry their dead and wounded. The house was deserted. Evidently the full compliment of armed men had been down at the beach.

The two G-men forced their captives to tie each other up, and then made the rounds to be sure the bonds were secure. Kerrigan went to the phone and called the F.B.I. Field Office, and ordered a couple of cars out on the double quick to pick up the prisoners.

"Better send a doctor, too," he said. "A couple of these birds need medical care." He paused a moment, then said, "Now get this. There'll be a submarine pulling in close to the shore here in a few minutes. Get a patrol of bombers in the air to take care of the baby—but not till *after* it has unloaded."

"How many men do you expect the submarine to unload?" the agent at the field office asked.

"I don't know," Kerrigan told him. "But we'll take a census for you. Phone the nearest Coast Guard barracks and have them send over a detail of men. We want to capture as many of the Nazis alive as we can. Klaw and I have an idea."

"Okay," said the agent.

"What about Dan Murdoch?" Kerrigan asked.

"Not a word from him, Johnny," the agent said. "We don't know what happened to him."

Kerrigan hung up glumly. He went back into the room where Klaw was guarding the prisoners.

"They haven't heard from Dan yet," he announced.

"Steve received the news in silence. By unspoken agreement, these three never indulged in any sort of worrying about each other—out loud. They knew that when fate finally caught up with them, there was nothing to do about it but accept it philosophically. They knew that if Murdoch hadn't contacted the field office by this time, something must have happened to him. They would have preferred, of course, to have it happen when they were all together, so they could go down fighting, shoulder to shoulder, and check out in each other's company. But if this was the way it had to be, then they could take it, with the resolve to make the enemy pay dearly.

The Coast Guard contingent arrived in twelve minutes, with a huge searchlight truck and two jeeps. They were none too soon, for lights blinked out at sea, and a few moments later they discerned a boat pulling for shore. It turned out to contain nine Nazis in civilian clothes, who meekly raised their hands in the air when they were suddenly confronted by the Coast Guard.

A FEW minutes later they were all treated to the impressive sight of two squadrons of medium bombers roaring out over the sea, and dropping flares over a half-mile-square area of water. The black hulk of the submarine became visible, a mile off shore. It was caught in the act of crash-diving, and the depth-charges rocked the coast as that under-sea craft was blasted into oblivion. Inside the house, where a squad of F.B.I. men had taken charge, Stephen Klaw and Johnny Kerrigan sat in the library with the Director and one of the Nazis, a young fellow of about Klaw's general build. They had picked him out of the group of captured saboteurs as the most likely prospect. A half hour in a private room with Johnny Kerrigan had been enough to take the starch out of him, and he was ready to co-operate fully with the authorities, in the hope that his life would be spared.

Just as in the case of other groups of saboteurs who had been caught, the government had difficulty in keeping them all from offering to squeal on their pals in order to escape the rope.

Though they had been well-trained for their deadly work, they had learned nothing in their Nazi schools about honor.

This particular Nazi's name was Helmut Goermann, and he spilled his guts to save his life.

"We came here to serve the Flaming Arrow," he said. His English was good, for he had been brought to this country as a child, afforded an American education, then had been taken back to Nazi-land to top it off with an education in mass murder.

"What we are to do for the Flaming Arrow, we do not know, nor do we know where he hides. But I can tell you how we are supposed to contact him. See, we are each given an identity disc with a Flaming Arrow on it. We must go at certain appointed times for each of us to a music store on Fourteenth Street. There we give a password and our number, and we receive instructions."

Kerrigan and Klaw exchanged glances. Then they looked over at the table where the possessions of Helmut Goermann were laid out. He had been well equipped for his work, with typical Nazi thoroughness. He had a small box of nitroglycerine tablets, a dagger, several pencil bombs, and a Lüger.

Klaw looked at the Director. "It's a shame, sir," he said, "that Helmut Goermann should fail to report at that music store. They'll be disappointed if he doesn't show up."

The Director's eyes twinkled. "You want to go in his place, of course?"

"Now wait a minute!" said Johnny Kerrigan. "Why should *he* go? There's a couple of big strapping Nazis in this bunch. *I* could impersonate one of them—"

"Nix," said Steve. "I thought of it first!"

CHAPTER 5
THE DECISION

STEPHEN KLAW walked slowly across Fourteenth Street, carrying a brief-case. It was exactly nine o'clock when he came to Moncore's Radio and Phonograph Shop.

A dark-haired, white-faced girl was playing records on a phonograph just inside. Klaw stopped and joined the half-dozen persons who were standing outside, listening. He waited till the record was finished, then went into the store. It was quite a large store, well equipped, with several salesmen waiting on customers. Along the walls there were racks holding thousands of phonograph records. At the rear, there were several sound-proof booths where one might listen to selections before buying them.

Klaw stopped beside the dark-haired girl.

"Yes, sir," she said. "Is there anything I can do for you?"

"Why yes. I would like to buy the *Toreador Song* from *Carmen.*"

Her eyes flickered suddenly, as he mentioned the song. "You—you wouldn't know offhand what number it is in the catalogue, would you?"

"Certainly," said Steve Klaw. "It's number 79."

"That's an expensive record."

"Nothing is too expensive for our purpose," Steve said. He took a disc from his pocket. On one side of it was pasted a bit of paper upon which was drawn a picture of an arrow. The arrow was drawn in blue pencil, and there were flames rising from its tip, drawn in red.

"You see," he said, "I can pay for it." He turned the disc over. On the other side was another bit of paper. Attached to the paper was a small snapshot of Stephen Klaw, and underneath it the number, 79.

The girl nodded swiftly. "I have just what you want," she said. "Follow me, please!"

She went to one of the racks, and took a record from the back of the pile. No one in the store paid them any attention as they went toward the rear.

"You may take it into Booth One and play it," she said.

Klaw took the record from her, entered the booth, and carefully closed the door behind him. He took the record from the container, placed it on the phonograph turntable, and started it.

Immediately, a voice began to come from the speaker. It was a low voice, but brittle and clear, with a clipped, authoritative tone:

"Orders for Number Seventy-nine. You have been sent here at great expense from the Fatherland to perform a specific task for me, the Flaming Arrow. The nature of that task has been kept secret from you until now, so that if you were captured immediately after being landed from the U-boat, you would have nothing to reveal. But now I shall tell you what you are to do. You will find instructions on the reverse side of this record. When you have memorized the instructions, destroy the record. If you should, by any chance, be arrested with this disc in your possession, let it drop to the floor. It is made of especially brittle material, and will immediately crumble into a thousand

bits. Remember, Number Seventy-nine, that you are on probation until you have accomplished this first task. If you succeed, you shall be given a chance to participate in the Grand Campaign for which you were really sent here—the campaign which will destroy American war power entirely. But if you should be captured in the performance of this first assignment, remember you could attain no greater honor than to lay down your life for the Fuehrer. Heil Hitler!"

THE VOICE ceased speaking, and the needle scratched along the record for a moment until the phonograph stopped automatically.

Klaw's eyes were glittering. He turned the record over, and started the phonograph going.

This time, another voice emerged from the speaker. It was a woman's voice, soft and cultured, with a distinct English accent:

"Number Seventy-nine Your first task will be the assassination of a man. It should not be difficult to accomplish, as this man does not expect attack, and is easy to reach. His name is Professor Ernst Swenson. He is a teacher of applied chemistry at Corbin University. This man fled from Europe at the time that our Fuehrer took power. He has since devoted himself to perfecting several inventions which will be dangerous to the Reich if placed in American hands. He must die, tonight. You will go to his laboratory in Carlyle Hall at the college, and say that you are an inventor in need of advice. He is always willing to help young inventors, and he will take you into his study. Once there, you will stab him to death, between the shoulder blades. He has a safe in his study. Use your nitro-glycerine tablets to blow the safe, and take therefrom the plans which you will

find. Have no fear of interruption, for we will have other men on the outside to protect you.

"When you leave the university, go out by the side door. A car will be waiting there, with a woman at the wheel. Throw the plans into the car, which will at once drive away. Make your escape, and come here tomorrow night for further instructions. Remember, you are now working for the Flaming Arrow. He brooks no failure, no excuses. We expect those plans tonight, before midnight. Memorize these instructions, and destroy this record. Heil Hitler!"

THE GLITTER was gone from Stephen Klaw's eyes as the woman's voice concluded the instructions. In its place there was a cold, bleak light. He took the record off the turntable, and placed it carefully in his brief-case. Out of the brief-case he took another phonograph record. This one he deliberately dropped to the floor.

He opened the door of the booth, and saw that the dark-haired girl was standing just outside, together with a stocky man who was apparently the manager.

Klaw said, "I'm so sorry. I dropped your record, and broke it."

He took out a five dollar bill, and offered it to the girl. She looked at the manager, who waved the bill aside.

"Do not think of it, my dear sir. It was an accident. I regret that we do not have another record of the same song to sell you. Perhaps you will come tomorrow night? We shall try to have another record for you.".

"Thank you," said Klaw. "I will be here tomorrow evening—if all goes well."

Klaw nodded to both of them, and hurried from the store.

Outside, he saw a taxicab cruising at the curb. He cast only a single glance at it, and hopped in.

The driver of the cab was a big, redheaded fellow. He nodded, and swung the cab away from the curb, fed her gas, and raced east, then swung north. After a couple of blocks he slowed down.

"We're being tailed," he said.

Klaw nodded. "I expected it, Johnny. It looks like I've been given my first assignment. Guess what."

Johnny Kerrigan shrugged. "Nothing less than murder, I'd say,"

"Right on the nose, Mope. I'm supposed to stab Professor Ernst Swenson to death, and rifle his safe. It's a sort of test assignment. If I make good, they'll let me in on the Grand Campaign."

"Ouch!" said Kerrigan. "And you've got to make good, or else all our spade-work goes for nothing!"

For several minutes they drove in silence, while Kerrigan made several turns, working north toward Corbin. Klaw glanced in the rear vision mirror and spotted two cars which were tailing them. One was a small panelled truck, the other a black coupé.

Klaw sighed. "They're going to watch every step I make from now on, Johnny. If I don't kill Professor Swenson, I'll never get in on the Grand Campaign!"

"Maybe you could go in to Swenson's and talk to him, and explain just why you have to stab him. Maybe Swenson would agree to let you stick a knife a couple of inches into him, just to make it look real."

"Nix," said Steve. "That dame who spoke on the record said

that the Flaming Arrow would accept no excuses or alibis. It has to be the real thing, Johnny. Either I kill Professor Swenson, or I give up any hope of working my way into the Flaming Arrow's organization!"

"That's a tough decision to have to make, Steve," said Johnny Kerrigan. "I don't envy you. No, I don't envy you at all!"

CHAPTER 6
BLOOD AND FLAME

CARLYLE HALL was the northernmost building on the Corbin University Campus. Kerrigan pulled to a stop, and Klaw got out. He saw that the small truck had already stopped, about a hundred feet back, and the coupé had passed them, but was making a U turn up at the end of the street.

Klaw went through the motions of paying the cab fare. "Watch that brief-case I left in the back. It has the record in it. Better get it down to the F.B.I. office fast, and have copies made of it on a recorder. Some day we may be able to convict the Flaming Arrow by his voice."

"*If* we catch him!" Kerrigan growled. Then he added, "Watch yourself, Shrimp. I smell something phony in the whole setup. I wish Dan Murdoch was here to keep an eye on you, but he won't get in till tomorrow morning. So watch your own back."

"What the devil will I do about Professor Swenson?" Steve demanded, while he ostensibly waited for Kerrigan to count out change. "I can't kill the old man in cold blood. And if I don't, I lose my 'in' with the Flaming Arrow."

"Don't worry about it," Kerrigan said. "You'll think of something when you get in there. And I'll be around to lend you moral support. I'll hide the brief-case under my seat, and pull the cab around in back. I'll stick around till you come out."

"A great help *you* are!" Klaw grumbled. He took his change and left the cab, going into Carlyle Hall.

The long corridor within was dim and cool. On either side there were numbered laboratories, each the sanctum of one of the science professors. The bulletin board said that Professor Swenson occupied Number Nine, and Steve went down the hall until he reached that door.

Klaw's mind was a miasma of indecision as he pressed the bell and waited for the door to be opened. He had a long, wicked knife in a sheath under his coat. But it was unthinkable that he should use the knife on the defenseless old professor of chemistry.

On the other hand, his duty was clear and sharp. This was war—total war, with civilians and soldiers alike under the constant threat of death. No one man's life—whether civilian or soldier—must be allowed to stand in the way of the country's safety.

Klaw shuddered. It was a dreadful decision to make. A Jap or a Nazi wouldn't have hesitated. But Stephen Klaw was a civilized man; and as he heard the footsteps within approaching the door in answer to his ring, he felt his blood growing cold.

Abruptly, the door was opened.

For a moment he stared at the tall, gorgeously beautiful girl who appeared there. He had expected to see a stoop-shoulder, elderly man. Instead, he was greeted by this blonde goddess.

"Good evening," he said. "I—I was looking for Professor Swenson."

The girl didn't smile. There was a strange, tight glint in her blue eyes, and she was holding herself taut, as if laboring under some great emotional strain.

"I'm Hildegarde Swenson," she said. "The Professor's niece. Come in, please. He's in the laboratory. He'll see you in a moment."

She escorted him across the study, and knocked at the door of the laboratory. A voice bade him enter.

"So you are an inventor, eh?" the Professor said, after Steve had introduced himself, giving a fictitious name. "And what can I do for you, young man?"

Steve was about to reply, but he frowned as he heard a tapping sound from somewhere underneath the floor.

"It is some men working on the basement," Swenson said. "Pay no attention to it."

HE TURNED his back on Steve for a moment, and stooped over his desk, reaching for a cigarette. It was as if he were deliberately inviting the knife in the back.

"Look here, Professor," Steve said suddenly. "I'm not an inventor at all. I've got to talk to you."

Swenson turned to look at him quizzically. "So?"

"I've been sent here to murder you, Professor. Don't be alarmed, I'm not going to do it. I'm a G-man. I need your cooperation to lay a devilish Nazi spy by the heels. I'm going to ask you to play dead. Will you do it?"

For a moment, Swenson was silent, studying Steve. And in that silence, the tapping from underneath continued....

Steve put both hands in his coat pockets.

The Professor smiled. "What is your real name, young man?"

"Stephen Klaw."

"Ah! You are one of the famous Suicide Squad."

"Well, that's what they call us."

"Tell me, Mr. Klaw—how did you come to discover all this about this—er—Flaming Arrow?"

"We caught a whole covey of Nazis out on Long Island," Steve explained. "And we sank a submarine. But wait till we tie into the Flaming Arrow himself!"

I am sure that will be interesting!" Professor Swenson murmured.

As he spoke he reached to the desk, and his finger moved toward a red button there.

Klaw took an automatic out of his right hand coat pocket.

"Don't push that button, Mr. Flaming Arrow!" he ordered.

Swenson froze. He stood like that for a moment, staring at Klaw. "What makes you think *I* am the Flaming Arrow?"

Steve smiled. "That tapping we hear is Morse code. You've got Murdoch down under this trap door, and he's been telling me about you!"

Swenson's finger still hovered over the button. "So the Suicide Squad thinks it has bested the Flaming Arrow, eh? I've tested every one of my new agents by ordering them to come here and attempt to kill me. If they go through with it, I know they're the right material. You see, I wear a bullet-proof vest."

Klaw grinned. "That's why the orders are to stab you between the shoulder-blades!"

"Exactly. And now, my dear Klaw, the jig may be up with me, personally. But my grand coup will go through on September first, anyway!"

"How so?"

"Because everything is set. Perhaps I will be dead, but the orders are all issued. My men are spread everywhere in the country, and on September first they will all act at a given moment. Water-power, utility plants, bomber factories, mines—all will be destroyed in a moment of time. And there's nothing you can do to stop it. Every name of every agent is in this building. And this building is going up in a terrific blast within thirty seconds!"

Klaw grinned. "Murdoch has been tapping the story up to me. The building won't be exploded unless you press that red button. And you're not going to press, it!"

Swenson thrust his hand down at the button…

STEPHEN KLAW fired three times fast, and every shot smashed into Swenson's arm, driving it back from the button, so that when his hand landed on the desk it was almost six inches from the danger spot. Swenson's face became twisted into a mask of ghastly hate. He fell, screaming something in a foreign language. And whether it was in response to those screamed orders, or as a result of the shots, a panel in the laboratory wall swung open, and a group of the vicious Korean knife-men erupted into the room.

Klaw's other gun came out of his pocket, and he smashed ten shots so swiftly into the massed knife-men that they all sounded like one continuous explosion. The room thundered with the reverberating gunfire as the Koreans were driven back, leaving the floor littered with dead and wounded. But others were pressing in from behind.

Klaw reached over and yanked at the wire along the desk, connecting with the red button. At least now the explosive could not be detonated by remote control. He stooped and yanked at the trapdoor in the middle of the floor. It opened, revealing the ladder which led into the darkness below.

He heard the sounds of a battle going on down there, of men fighting desperately in the dark, and then he was overwhelmed by a second rush of the Koreans. There were many more of them now and their gleaming knives slashed at Steve as their weight carried him over the edge of the trapdoor opening.

They landed in a heap, and Steve pushed up to his feet. For a moment he was free of his clinging enemies in the darkness, but others were dropping down after him, and he heard gunfire far down at the other end.

Then a voice was raised in a stentorian shout: "*This way, Shrimp!*"

Steve's eyes widened. That voice was Johnny Kerrigan's!

But he didn't bother to wonder how Johnny had got in there. He raced through the darkness toward the voice.

Suddenly an arrow hummed through the darkness, struck a wall, and burst into flame. By its light, Steve saw the cell doors which he had passed. They were open, and the cells untenanted. But at the far end of the cellar, he saw Kerrigan and Murdoch. Ammunition cases were piled high all around them, and Murdoch was firing at a small group of bowmen all the way over to the right, while Kerrigan was trying to boost a boy up through a high, narrow window.

Kerrigan got the boy through just as Steve Klaw joined them. Arrows were humming past his head, thudding into the ammunition cases and bursting into flame. Kerrigan stepped past him and brought his two revolvers into play at Murdoch's side, firing into the bowmen who were now almost invisible, for they had retreated beyond the area of light from the burning arrows.

Klaw swiftly inserted new clips in his automatics, then hurried around to the cases, striking off the flaming arrows with the butts of his guns. Then, when Murdoch emptied his guns, he was relieved by Klaw, who took his place at Kerrigan's side while Dan reloaded.

Kerrigan took his turn at fighting the arrows, and shouted to Klaw, "I heard Dan's Morse code out in back, Shrimp, so I shot the grating away from this window and broke in. It looks like it'll be tough to break out, though!"

"They've got to run out of those damned arrows some time!" Murdoch yelled.

JUST THEN they heard a grunt from Johnny Kerrigan, and then a yell. They turned around for just a fraction of a second, and saw Johnny locked in a death struggle with one of the Koreans who had slipped in through the high window. The fellow had a gleaming knife, with which he was trying to drive an upward stab at Johnny's stomach.

Kerrigan caught the fellow's wrist, yanked him forward, caught him by one foot, and still holding on to the hand he began spinning around. The Korean shrieked as he went whirling through the air, held by one wrist and one ankle. Klaw and Murdoch dropped flat on the floor, and Kerrigan let go of the fellow. He went sailing out into the darkness where his fellow bowmen were, and an arrow struck him, then burst into flames. The unfortunate Korean thudded to the floor.

The flame illuminated the rest of the cellar, showing the G-men what a shambles the place had become. Dead Koreans lay all over. The Suicide Squad's shooting had been pretty effective, but they hadn't been able to see the result. Now they saw that barely a half-dozen of the Koreans were still in the fight. And when the Koreans saw that their numbers had been so terribly depleted, they quit cold and went scrambling up the ladder to safety.

But they had waited just a little too long. The police and the fire department were outside in force to welcome them.

Not a single one of them escaped.

Twenty minutes later the fire in the cellar was under control, and the ammunition boxes had been sufficiently wetted down so they wouldn't explode.

Professor Swenson, alias the Flaming Arrow, was in custody, with one shattered arm. All the records in the building were being examined by a hastily convened staff of F.B.I. men.

That night, raids took place in every city where an agent of the Flaming Arrow was located. All the next day a dreary procession of surprised and bewildered Nazis were marched into federal courts for arraignment and promise of a speedy trial and execution.

It was almost six o'clock before Kerrigan and Murdoch and Klaw got through signing complaints and affidavits in the various courts having jurisdiction.

Murdoch's hand was still bandaged, so he was spared the writing, but Steve and Johnny had to do that much extra, while Dan sat on the edge of a desk, watching them with a sardonic smile.

"All right, Mope," Steve said, tossing down his pen. "We're all through. Let's go!"

They hurried out the side way of the Supreme Court, in order to avoid the reporters and photographers. Hildegarde and Holgar were waiting for them there.

"Let's snap it up," said Steve. "There's a bus leaving in twenty minutes for Virginia Beach. We can hire a boat tomorrow morning, and go deep-sea fishing. We got a two-day leave."

Hildegarde's face was flushed, and her eyes were at peace for the first time. Little Holgar was capering excitedly.

But just then a Capitol messenger came hurrying down the street after them.

"Mr. Kerrigan!"

Frowning, Johnny stopped. The messenger said breathlessly, "They sent me after you. Congress is voting you three men a medal, and they want you to come right over for the ceremony!"

"Aw, gee," said Holgar. "No fishing!"

But Kerrigan and Murdoch and Klaw stood looking at

each other for a moment. Kerrigan was the first to nod. Then Murdoch nodded. Steve Klaw grinned.

"So be it, Mopes!" he said.

Then the three of them got hold of Hildegarde's and Holgar's arm, and began walking swiftly—not toward the Hall of Congress, but in the direction of the bus for the fishing trip!

"What good's a medal?" said Murdoch. "You can't take it with you!"

BLOOD, SWEAT AND BULLETS

CHAPTER 1
IT'S TIME TO DIE!

A T THE corner of Forty-second Street and Fifth Avenue
in the City of New York, Stephen Klaw stood, waiting to
be shot to death.

It was now three minutes before noon. At twelve o'clock
exactly, a steel-jacketed slug from a silenced .30-.40 Winchester
rifle would come whining down from one of the hundreds of
windows in the office buildings opposite, and would smash its
way into Stephen Klaw's heart.

It was raining, and it was chilly. The rain was coming down
slantwise in lashing slabs of fury, and the wind was blowing from
the north, both trying to discourage the hurrying Christmas
shoppers. Many of them had taken shelter in the Public Library,
and others stood in the doorways of office buildings—in one
of which lurked an expert marksman with his eye glued to the
telescopic sight. The shot would be a difficult one, due to the
wind and the rain. But Klaw knew that the marksman—wherever he was or whoever he was—would not miss. Too much was
at stake for that.

He glanced at his wrist watch, pulling his hand from his overcoat pocket for an instant. Two minutes of twelve. The second

hand was moving around swiftly on the start of its next-to-last lap. Two full revolutions around the dial, and the shot would come. No sooner, no later. That was the essence of German thoroughness with which this execution was to be consummated.

Klaw put his hand back in his pocket.

That bullet, when it *did* come, would not be intended for Stephen Klaw. It was earmarked for another man. But Klaw was taking the intended victim's place. For the next two minutes, Klaw was—to all intents and purposes—one, Kurt Siglith.

Kurt Siglith was of the same build as Stephen Klaw. And now, with hat-brim turned down and coat collar pulled up around his chin, Klaw knew that the marksman would surely believe he was firing at Kurt Siglith—especially since these were Siglith's brown hat and brown overcoat, and since Klaw was standing directly in front of the northerly stone lion guarding the Public Library entrance, exactly where Siglith was supposed to be standing at this time.

The irony of it was that Kurt Siglith was nobody of great importance. He was a minor cog in the Nazi spy-machine which the F.B.I. had just got wind of. Siglith was earmarked for liquidation. He was not supposed to know that this was an appointment with death. But he had learned it somehow, and he had gone, shivering in terror, to the Federal Bureau of Investigation.

Siglith's visit at that particular moment was like manna from heaven. For twenty days now, every agency of the United States had been working day and night, feverishly against time, to uncover a certain "secret" army which was known to be ready to go into action—*within the United States.*

THE LEADER of that secret army was known, but was as elusive as an eel. His name was Baron Oxenburg; but he was known from Berlin to Yokohama as "The Ox." There had been cautious rumors about The Ox. He had established himself in America, recruiting an army of shock troops which would deal a crippling blow to the United States upon a given date. Christmas Day was the date. And now it was the twentieth of December, and nothing had broken—until Siglith appeared.

Siglith's story was confused and almost hysterical. He had worked under cover for Oxenburg for twenty years; living here with false citizenship papers, working as an unassuming mechanic. But there was to be a purge, and Siglith was to be liquidated. This much he knew—that the appointment at the library meant death from a rifle bullet. So he had come to the F.B.I. to sell his secret. He told of certain coded plans for the Oxenburg Campaign—plans of which he had a copy, and which he would turn over at a price. The price was absolute guarantee of safety. Oxenburg must think him dead, and he must be given new papers which would enable him to live in anonymity, free of the terror of the purge.

All these things the government agreed to do—even to making it seem that Siglith died.

And so today, Stephen Klaw was standing at the library, and Siglith was to get a bullet in the heart—by proxy! Somewhere in one of those tall office buildings whose windows looked down through the rain upon the figure of Stephen Klaw in his brown hat and overcoat, there was an expert marksman. And, spread out over the entire area surrounding the Public Library there were two hundred agents of the Department of Justice, and as many plainclothesmen of the New York City Police Department. They were watching like hawks for the tell-tale curl of smoke which would emanate from the rifle breech when the shot was fired. When Stephen Klaw died at twelve o'clock, they would capture the killer. And they would have the first concrete lead to the dangerous underground army of Baron Oxenburg. Klaw was trading his life for a chance to strike at a dangerous enemy of the nation.

There were only two other men in the F.B.I. to whom such an assignment might have been given. They were Stephen Klaw's partners in the Suicide Squad—Dan Murdoch and Johnny Kerrigan. That was the kind of job the Suicide Squad always got. They never rated the ordinary routine assignments involving investigations, or the tracking down of minor embezzlers. They asked for and got only those jobs from which there was hardly any chance of returning alive.

Once again, Klaw looked at his wrist watch. Another minute was gone. Sixty seconds more to go. Calmly, he lit a cigarette, cupping the flame against the rain and wind, and being careful, also, to hide his face. His hand was steady as he flicked the match away. He exhaled a thick cloud of smoke from his nostrils, and glanced across the Avenue toward a parked car at the opposite curb, in which two men were seated.

Big, blond Johnny Kerrigan was at the wheel of that car. His powerful hands had a strangle-hold on the rim, and he was chewing his lower lip, and his haggard eyes never left the slim figure of Stephen Klaw. Next to Johnny Kerrigan sat Dan Murdoch, whose dark and handsome face was now drawn into the tight lines of a carved obelisk.

"We shouldn't have let the Shrimp do it, Johnny!" Murdoch groaned. "There's still time. Let's get him away from there!"

Johnny Kerrigan gripped the wheel more tightly, as if preventing himself from getting out and running over to Klaw. "The Shrimp won the toss, didn't he?" Kerrigan demanded harshly. "Suppose you'd won the toss—would you want Steve or me to drag you away from there right now?"

"No," said Dan Murdoch. "No." His face was white. "But I can't stand it, Johnny. I can't stand sitting here and watching the Shrimp get killed in cold blood. I—I would feel better if I were over there instead of him."

"So would I," growled Johnny. "But it had to come sometime. Today it's Steve. Tomorrow it'll be you and me, Dan. We've lived too long anyway."

It was true. They had lived too long on this job. Two years ago, there had been five on the Suicide Squad. Today there were only three. At noon, there would be but two. Tomorrow there might be none. There were strange tales in the underworld about the Suicide Squad—tales that had become almost legendary. It was said that Kerrigan and Murdoch and Klaw seemed always to *look* for death, yet never to find it. Perhaps because they did not fear the Grim Old Man, they were immune. But today—today the Suicide Squad was going to take it on the chin. Today, for the first time, they would meet death without a fight.

Murdoch looked at his wrist watch. "Thirty seconds to go, Johnny!"

STEPHEN KLAW was also looking at his watch. He would rather not have looked. He preferred to have the death bullet come unexpectedly. But he had studied Kurt Siglith's manner-isms, and had found that Siglith was a nervous man. One of his habitual nervous motions was to look constantly at his wrist watch. So Steve did the same. That killer—wherever he might be—would surely never doubt that this was his man.

Rain trickled down from Steve's hat-brim onto his upturned coat collar as he watched the second-hand. Twenty-five seconds—twenty seconds—fifteen—seven....

He looked up from the watch, and started to make a farewell gesture to Kerrigan and Murdoch across the street—and a girl came leaping out of a convertible coupé which had screamed to a stop on hotly-braked tires at the curb directly in front of Stephen Klaw.

There was a flash of shapely, silk-clad legs as she jumped to the sidewalk. Klaw got a blurred, rain-obscured vision of a tautly beautiful face, dark, bobbed hair and a pair of big, frantic eyes. She wore no hat, and the rain had tangled and matted her hair. She was shouting, "Quick, Siglith! They'll kill you—"

And then she was upon him, and had seized the lapels of his coat, and was frantically, furiously trying to drag him around in back of the stone lion.

"A rifle!" she gasped. "They'll shoot! They're going to—"

Steve's watch showed one second before noon.

He seized the girl's hands, yanked them away from his lapels, and thrust her to one side. "You little fool—"

"No, no!" she screamed, and lunged at him. Her weight carried him back a half step. "They'll kill—"

She said no more.

BLOOD, SWEAT AND BULLETS

He pulled the wheel even farther
back, gauging his distance
with uncanny accuracy....

Something whined, high and shrill in the air.

Desperately, Steve tried to swing the girl around. But it was too late. There was the terrible *thump* of hard metal spatting into human flesh. The girl was catapulted into Steve's arms by the tremendous impact of the steel-jacketed projectile, and they were both hurled backward against the stone lion. The girl became stiff in Steve's arms, and blood spurted out over her fur coat from a wound below the right breast.

Almost simultaneously, men seemed to materialize on all sides, as if from nowhere—grim, lean-jawed F.B.I. agents, and hard-bitten city detectives. They surrounded Steve and the girl, not knowing for the moment, which had been hit.

At the same time, other agents began to converge in grim array, toward the Volt Building, several hundred yards away. Keen eyes had spotted the spurt of smoke. They knew where the rifleman was. In less than half a minute the Volt Building was surrounded. Escape would be impossible. Tear gas guns appeared in the hands of the F.B.I. men as they flooded into the building, pre-empting the elevators, and moving bleakly up to the fifth floor. They were going to capture that rifleman alive. None of them knew that Stephen Klaw was still alive, for they hadn't been able to see the girl take the slug intended for him. They were resolved that they would not fail to make this rifleman talk—Stephen Klaw should not have died in vain....

CHAPTER 2
MERRY OX-MAS!

IN ROOM 512 of the Volt Building, a young man with dark hair and sensitive, clean-cut features, knelt at the window with a rifle at his shoulder.

The gun had recoiled from the shot he had just fired, and a thin wisp of smoke was trickling upward from it. But the young man remained immovable for a full twenty seconds after pulling the trigger. His eyes were fixed upon the hurrying throng which had crowded around Stephen Klaw and the dark girl, far down there in front of the Public Library.

He could no longer see either Klaw or the girl. But he did see the grim men who suddenly came hurrying from every direction toward this building, and in whose hands there had now appeared tear gas guns and bombs.

His sensitive lips twitched into a hopeless little smile. Then the smile faded. With a sudden gesture of revulsion, he threw the costly rifle to the floor, and got to his feet. He turned around and faced the bare room, in which there was only a desk, a chair and a telephone.

"*I killed him!*" he kept repeating under his breath in a deadly monotone. "*I killed him. I'm a murderer!*"

He picked up the telephone. His hand shook so that he was barely able to dial his number. He closed his eyes tightly, as if to shut out the sight of the thing he had done. When he got his connection, he said: "This is Gregor. Well, I've done it. I've killed him."

His knuckles whitened with the intensity of his grip on the phone. A smooth, suave voice trickled through from the receiver—a voice which somehow gave the impression of a sinuous, snake-like owner without human feeling or compassion.

"Excellent, my dear Gregor. I knew that you would not fail. You are to be commended on your marksmanship. I wish it were possible for me to give you another medal to add to your many shooting trophies. However, trust me, I shall find a suitable reward—"

"Damn you!" young Gregor choked. "Stop that. I want no reward from you—only that you should keep your promise—about Ninovna. You—you—" he gulped, then demanded eagerly, almost piteously, "She'll be—all right now? Nothing will happen to her?"

"Of course, my dear Gregor. Nothing will happen to her—provided you leave no clue for the Americans. Remember, your work is only half done. The other half consists of making a clean getaway."

Gregor laughed harshly. "Impossible. The Federal agents were watching. They must have been tipped off. They saw the smoke from the rifle. They're on the way up, now."

The voice at the other end became suddenly cold, harsh. "You mean you cannot escape?"

"That's right."

There was a pause. Then, "Gregor, you must not fall into the hands of the Americans. You understand?"

"I understand. I won't. Only I must be sure that Ninovna—that nothing will happen to her. My sister—Lola—tried to save

Siglith. She got there just a minute ago. She must have found out, somehow. But—but you mustn't hold that against me—or Ninovna."

"I will hold nothing against you, Gregor—as long as the G-Men find no clue."

"They won't!" Gregor said grimly, and hung up.

Already, grim men were in the corridor. He heard a voice say, "Here—this is the room. Break the glass. Flood him with tear gas. Smoke him out—"

Gregor's face was white and drawn like that of an old man. He walked across the bare room with the stiff motions of a somnambulist. Behind him, the plate glass in the door was shattered by a gun butt. Men were shouting, calling to him to surrender. He paid no attention.

He reached the window, threw one leg over, then the other. He closed his eyes, and thrust himself out from the ledge. His body went plummeting out into space.

IN THE street, a thousand pairs of eyes were turned upward to watch in stunned fascination as a human being plummeted down, to be crushed against the concrete sidewalk into an unrecognizable, lifeless mass, locking within his bloody self the secret which the G-Men sought.

Traffic ceased, and all became quiet at this busiest intersection of the world, as if the entire universe had suddenly become converted into stone. The only movement was in the small but compact group in front of the library, surrounding Stephen Klaw, and the girl who had been shot.

Kerrigan and Murdoch, the first to reach them, were pawing unbelievingly at Klaw.

"Shrimp!" he whispered. "Are you really alive? I thought that slug got you—"

Steve was kneeling beside the girl. She was not dead. The bullet had penetrated her right side, and the wound was bleeding copiously. Her eyes were open, and she was looking up at Klaw, with a strange mixture of surprise and pain and terror in them.

"You—you're not Siglith!" she managed to gasp.

"No, my dear," Stephen Klaw said softly. "I was taking Siglith's place. And you took mine. You knew something-something that made you come here to try to stop a murder. Can you talk?"

It was at that moment that the thud of the falling body of the fair-haired young man brought them all to attention. One of the G-Men surrounding them exclaimed, "It's the killer! He jumped! He'll never talk!"

The girl almost jerked from Steve's arms. Her mouth twisted horribly, and she screamed through her pain. "My brother! Gregor! Dead! He—"

She fell back, unconscious. The blood continued to pulse from the wound under her breast, and her breath came in short, rasping intervals. Rain beat down, washing the crimson stain away as soon as it formed.

Steve glanced up hopelessly at Dan and Johnny.

"A hospital! We've got to get her to a hospital!"

Looking around swiftly, he saw that the G-Men were surrounding them in such a way that none of the passersby could see what was going on. He motioned to Murdoch, who bent and took the limp body of the girl from his arms. Then Steve swiftly stripped off his coat and hat—the coat and hat of Kurt Siglith. He wrapped the coat around the girl, pressed the hat on her head.

"Let Oxenburg think his killer succeeded in getting Siglith! Get an ambulance. Take her to a hospital. Keep her under guard every minute of the day and night!"

A little man pushed through the crowd of G-Men, carrying a small medical bag.

"I'm a doctor!" he called out. "I'm a doctor. Can I help?"

He pushed through, and blinked when he saw the girl lying in the rain, with a man's brown coat thrown over her.

Klaw, watching the man keenly, saw his lips compress as he knelt beside her and set to work with capable fingers. And just then, an ambulance clanged to a stop at the curb.

The doctor was ripping away the girl's clothes from the wound when the ambulance interne and the driver appeared with a stretcher.

Stephen Klaw said, "Thanks, doctor," to the little man. "You needn't bother now. The interne will take care of her."

The doctor scowled, and looked up at him. "See here, don't you butt in. This girl requires immediate attention. My office is in the Brooks Building, right across the street. Take her in there."

"Never mind, doctor," Steve said. "We'll take her to the hospital."

The little man persisted, "You're trifling with her life—"

Steve signalled to Johnny Kerrigan, who took the little doctor by the arm and dragged him to one side. The interne and the ambulance driver lifted the unconscious body to the stretcher. Steve wrapped the brown coat around her.

"Get her in there, fast!" he ordered. "And don't let anyone see who she is. She's to be registered as Kurt Siglith. Remember that. There'll be a couple of men stationed outside her room at all times, and no one is to be allowed to talk to her!"

The interne looked puzzled, but when he saw Steve's shield, he nodded briskly. "Right!"

The other agents kept close to the stretcher, preventing anyone in the street from glimpsing the girl.

THE AMBULANCE clanged off, with a uniformed patrolman and two Federal agents riding along. Across the street, a crowd was gathered around the body of the fair-haired young man. For him, there was to be no ambulance. The morgue-wagon would take *him* away. Dan Murdoch had hurried over there, and he was going through the young man's clothes, seeking some kind of identification. Johnny Kerrigan was still holding on to the arm of the little doctor whom he had dragged away from the wounded girl. Steve came over to them. The little doctor exclaimed fussily, "See here, this man—" indicating Johnny—"tells me that you are agents of the Department of Justice. I—er—didn't know that. I thought you were merely a stranger, interfering. Of course, if you had a special reason for wanting that girl taken to the hospital instead of to my office—"

"Yes, doctor," Steve said mildly. "We had a special reason. Just forget about the whole thing, doctor—"

"Selden," the other supplied. "Doctor Philip Selden. My card."

Steve took the card, glanced at it carelessly, rubbed a thumb over the type, and thrust it in his pocket. He lifted up his thumb, and frowned at a black smudge on it.

"If you please, Doctor Selden," he requested, "I must ask you to keep this whole thing quiet. Don't mention the fact that the girl was wounded. You see, the murderer may think he killed a man, not the girl. We want him to remain under that delusion."

"Of course," Selden assented readily. "Glad to help the F.B.I. And now—er—if you'll excuse me, I must be getting along."

He smiled vaguely at Johnny Kerrigan, flashed a quick glance at Steve, and headed briskly across the street toward the Brook Building where he had said his office was located.

Just then, Dan Murdoch came over from across the street, where he had been going through the dead rifleman's pockets. He shook his head. "Not a thing on him. Not even a laundry mark. We might have expected that."

One of the agents who had been examining the roadster in which the girl had driven up, came over with a purse. "Here's her bag. Plenty of identification. Driver's license, address book, Traveler's Cheques. Her name's Lola Pavlov—"

But Steve wasn't listening. He took Kerrigan and Murdoch each by the arm. "Hang on here, Mopes," he whispered, swiftly. "I'll be right back!" And he slipped between them, and started off after Doctor Selden.

"Wait a minute, Shrimp!" Murdoch growled. "How about letting us in on some fun—"

"No time now," Klaw called back. "This is a hot hunch!"

Selden was already half-way across the street. Klaw hurried

after him, and saw the doctor enter the Brooks Building, diagonally opposite. The doctor threw a hasty glance behind him before going in, but the milling throng prevented him from noticing Klaw.

Steve swung into the lobby almost on the doctor's heels, and saw the little man vanish up the stairs at the rear. He glanced at the bulletin board, and saw that Selden's office was on the seventh floor—709. He frowned. Why would the doctor prefer to *walk* up seven flights, instead of taking the elevator?

And then he saw the answer. The two elevator cages which served the building were at rest here on the main floor, with the doors open, and no operators in evidence. The elevator boys must have deserted their posts in favor of the morbid scene outside.

Klaw's eyes flickered. He entered the nearest of the cages, closed the door, and pulled the lever over. The cage shot upward, and he stopped it at the seventh floor. He got out, well ahead of Doctor Selden, who had probably not even reached the second floor yet.

STEVE HURRIED down the hall until he came to the frosted-glass panel of 709. The modest lettering on the glass proclaimed that this was the office of Philip Selden, M.D., Consultations By Appointment Only.

Steve tried the door, and found it locked. Glancing around to make sure he was not observed, he took out his kit of skeleton keys, and tried them swiftly, one after the other. He worked hastily, for there were only a few moments now before Selden would reach this floor. The third key clicked the lock. Steve pushed the door open and went in. He closed the door carefully behind him, and locked it. Then he looked around.

He was in a small waiting room. Beyond it, there was a consultation room, and he could see another door in there, which opened into the examining room, equipped with an X-ray, a fluoroscope, and a couple of therapeutic machines.

As he stood there, the phone on the desk, in the consultation room began to ring. At the same time, he heard hasty steps outside, and then a key being inserted in the lock. Selden had arrived.

Steve sprinted through the consultation office, into the examining room, and hid behind the fluoroscope frame. Peering out, he saw Selden come in, wiping sweat from his forehead. The phone was still emitting an, imperious clamor. Selden grimaced, and snatched it up.

"Doctor Selden speaking," he said.

Steve, peering from the semi-dark examining room, saw the little doctor's body become tense as an indistinguishable voice spoke softly through the transmitter. Selden's back was to the examining room, so Steve couldn't see his face, but he sensed the sudden subservient attitude which enveloped the doctor, and which trickled from his very voice.

"Yes, yes, I have a report for you. I—I saw Gregor jump. He jumped after firing the shot. Yes, he is dead. But—but there is something else. Something very startling—"

That was as much as Stephen Klaw waited to hear. He came out of the examining room like a rocket, and hit Selden in a tackle that sent the doctor smashing into the desk, with the phone flying out of his hand.

Selden never finished what he had been about to say into the phone. Instead, he uttered a sharp cry of anger, and shoved his hand into his coat pocket.

Stephen Klaw's eyes were cold and hard. He brought up his balled fist in a merciless, smashing blow squarely into Selden's jaw. There was a sickening thud, and the doctor's head snapped up. His body arched far back over the desk, and then he went limp. He slid down to the floor in an inert heap.

Klaw massaged his knuckles, then stooped and picked up the telephone.

"Good afternoon, Baron Oxenburg," he said.

For a moment there was silence. Then a cool, self-contained voice spoke through the receiver, barely above a whisper.

"Ah! This is not Selden. Who is this?"

"Stephen Klaw, at your service, Baron."

"Klaw? Ah, yes. I place the name. You are one of those three irresponsible madmen of the F.B.I.— the Suicide Squad!"

"Thank you."

"May I ask what you have done to Selden?"

"I think I broke his jaw."

"That is too bad. He had not finished his report. He was about to tell me some important news."

"I'll tell it to you, Baron. Gregor shot Siglith, as you know, and then committed suicide. But Siglith lived long enough to tell me everything he knew. Do you understand, Baron?"

"I understand, my dear Klaw, but I don't believe you."

"As a matter of fact, Baron, I know a good deal more than Siglith told me. For instance, I know about—Lola Pavlov!"

"Ah!" said Baron Oxenburg. "You compel me to take an interest in you, Mr. Klaw. I shall have to take measures to—er—eliminate you!"

"That," said Stephen Klaw, "is just what I wanted to accomplish!" And he hung up.

CHAPTER 3
PO BOX LT-13

KURT SIGLITH sat with his head in his hands. The real Kurt Siglith. In the spacious hotel suite which the F.B.I. had rented for him, there was little chance that any harm might come to him. Yet the fear was still in his bones.

He looked up when Stephen Klaw entered the room, and his eyes became wide, and he glanced around at the two F.B.I. guards who sat in the room with him. Then his gaze crept back to Klaw, and he said, "You—you're still alive? They—they didn't try to kill you?"

Klaw nodded grimly. "They tried, all right." The contempt in his voice was difficult to hide; contempt for this frightened traitor who valued his miserable life so highly.

Siglith came up from his chair in a convulsive jerk. "But—but you're still alive! Impossible. Oxenburg never makes a mistake. He meant me to be killed at noon today, and you were posing as me; therefore, you should be dead. The Ox never fails."

"It's all right," Steve Klaw said wearily. "Oxenburg thinks

you're dead. Lola Pavlov stepped in the way of the bullet. She's in the hospital now. But we let them think it was you. Lola is being smuggled out of the city, and a body from the morgue has been slipped into the hospital room. It'll be buried as you. Officially, you're dead, Siglith—just as you wanted."

Kurt Siglith clutched at Klaw's sleeve. "You're telling me the truth?" he demanded eagerly. "You—you're not lying to me?"

Steve made a gesture of distaste. From his pocket he took a leather wallet containing a passport and several official papers.

"Here are your new documents. From now on, you're Karl Stegner. We've created a whole new identity for you, just as you asked. You can travel anywhere in South America, now, without fear."

Siglith seized the documents, and thumbed through them eagerly. "Ah!" He seemed to grow perceptibly, as the shadow of terror was lifted off him.

"All right," Steve Klaw said crisply. "We've kept our part of the bargain, Siglith. Now you keep yours. Where are the plans of the Oxenburg campaign?"

Siglith sat weakly in the easy chair. He wiped perspiration from his forehead. "You will find the plans of the Oxenburg campaign in the General Post Office," he said.

"In the Post Office!" Steve exclaimed.

Siglith nodded. "When I realized that Oxenburg intended to have me killed sooner or later, I stole a copy of the plans and mailed them to a Post Office Box which I rented. They are waiting there to be picked up—Box Number LT-13."

Klaw's eyes flickered. "LT-13!" he repeated. He turned to the door. "After we've picked up the papers, you'll be paid off. Then you'll be free to go. You can travel to any part of the world you like, on that passport. Even Germany."

"Germany?" said Siglith. "What do you mean? You are at war with Germany—"

Klaw grinned. "I bet the Gestapo would send a special ship to give you passage back there. I bet they'd gladly stand the expense for a chance at making an example out of you!"

As he opened the door and stepped out of the room, he saw Siglith shuddering. A traitor's life is not a happy one—even a traitor to Nazi Germany. And Siglith was doubly a traitor. For twenty years he had lived in the United States, working for the German Foreign Service. For twenty years he had planned to betray the country which afforded him hospitality. And now he was betraying his native land. Somewhere in the world he might find peace of mind; but he'd have to go far and forget much.

DOWNSTAIRS IN the lobby, Johnny Kerrigan was making a purchase at the cigar counter, and Dan Murdoch was thumbing through the telephone directory at the phone booths.

Steve Klaw signaled unobtrusively to Kerrigan, and then moved over to the phone booths. As he passed Murdoch he said swiftly, "General Post Office, Mope. Box LT-13."

"Right, Shrimp!" said Murdoch. "Box LT-13. Meet you in a half hour, Johnny will stick with you."

Steve moved on past Murdoch, and entered one of the phone booths. Murdoch turned and headed toward the street exit, and Johnny Kerrigan remained in the lobby.

Inside the phone booth, Klaw dropped a nickel in the slot,

and dialed the private number of the F.B.I. Field Office. In a moment he was talking to the Director of the Federal Bureau of Investigation, who had flown in from Washington that morning.

"Everything running according to schedule so far, sir," Steve reported. "Siglith came through with the dope. If he's telling the truth, the stuff is at Box LT-13, General Post Office. Dan Murdoch is on his way there now, to pick it up. Better have him covered."

"I'll have a squad of men at the Post Office in a few minutes," the Director said, "And you and Johnny better come right in. If that stuff is really the coded plans of the Oxenburg Campaign, I'll have a job for you three."

"Right, sir," said Steve. He hung up and left the booth. He exchanged no word with Johnny Kerrigan, but hurried out of the lobby and flagged a cab. He gave the driver the address of the F.B.I. Field Office, and as the cab pulled away, he saw Johnny Kerrigan climb into another taxi behind him, to follow.

From the moment that Stephen Klaw had spoken to Oxenburg over the phone, they had expected that an attack of some kind would be made on Klaw. Oxenburg's organization in the United States was known and talked about in espionage quarters throughout the world. For almost a year now there had been cautious rumors about the army of shock troops which Baron Oxenburg had ready for the purpose of striking one mighty, crippling blow at the United States.

"The Ox" himself was as elusive as Satan, and more ruthless. Sometimes he was reported on the east coast, while at the same time there were stories that he had been seen in California or in Canada. It was certain that he had "nests" spotted all over the country, from which he could operate at will. Cunningly trunked-in telephone lines made it possible for him to speak with impunity over the telephone—as he had done to Gregor and Steve Klaw—without the danger of being traced. His agents were everywhere, many in the guise of United States citizens.

These agents were able to move about all over the country, unsuspected, just as Kurt Siglith had done for many years; and as a result Oxenburg had engineered many a minor coup by means of which he had provided arms and ammunition for his secret army. Only recently, Kerrigan and Murdoch and Klaw had come into possession of information which had led them to Kurt Siglith, and this was now the first concrete link to the Oxenburg Army.

But time was growing short. With the situation growing more tense by the hour on the European front, there was every indication that Germany would order the Oxenburg Army to strike. It was imperative to discover their plans, their dispositions, the points at which they would attack. Siglith had told them that the plans were written in code so that even now, with the plans almost in the grasp of the Federal agents, there was still the element of time necessary to break down whatever code it might be.

AT THE Department of Justice Building, where the Field Office was located, Klaw descended from the cab and paid off. Out of the corner of his eye he saw Johnny Kerrigan's cab pulling up about fifty feet behind, and Johnny getting out.

Lexington Avenue was busy at this time of day, with men

and women, in and out of uniform, hurrying in both directions. Steve turned away from the cab, and began to make his way across the sidewalk toward the building entrance, when a woman stopped him.

"Excuse me," she said. "Are you Stephen Klaw?"

Steve gazed at her admiringly. Her slender body was encased in a beautiful glossy black fur coat which was no blacker than her hair and her eyes. She was not smiling, and her face was almost entirely devoid of expression. But there was a subtle something in those black and secret eyes of hers which seemed to be trying to hide some grim and hideous truth.

"Yes," Steve said shortly. "I'm Klaw."

"I have something to tell you," she said. "About—the Oxenburg Plan!"

"Ah!" said Steve. "Who are you?"

"My name will mean little to you. My information much. You must promise to ask no questions, but to come with me and to listen, then to allow me to leave freely."

"Where do you want me to go with you?"

"I can't tell you that. You'll know when you get there."

"I have no time," Steve told her.

She smiled for the first time now, and it was not a pleasant smile. "Don't be a fool, Klaw. You're in a hurry, because you think you're going to lay your hands on the coded plan."

"Maybe I am," Klaw told her.

Her eyes nickered. "Then Siglith really *did* talk before he died!"

"Look here," Klaw said suddenly. "You've talked enough right now to lay yourself open to arrest. You've said enough so far, to put a noose around that pretty neck of yours. Now what's the game?"

Once more she smiled that secret smile of hers. "I'm sure you won't arrest me, Mr. Klaw. Yes, I'll admit that I know all about the Oxenburg Plan. But you won't arrest me."

"Why not?"

"Because as a prisoner of the United States, I'll be of no use to you whatsoever. But free—I may help you to avert the blow that Oxenburg is going to strike on Christmas Day."

"Wait!" She raised a hand as Steve was about to speak. "Listen well to me, Stephen Klaw. Maybe you're going to get hold of a copy of the Oxenburg Plan. But it won't do you any good. Those plans were drawn in code—a code that all your experts couldn't break in a month. And in five days, Christmas will be here. The secret you want is locked in the code, and Oxenburg will strike while your experts are still working on it!"

"Then you can help us break the code?" Steve asked. "You have the key?"

She shook her head. "I haven't the key. Only one man in the United States besides Baron Oxenburg has the key to that code. I can tell you where to find that man. Come with me and listen to my terms, and if you agree to them, I shall tell you what you need to know. But you must act now, or it will be forever too late!"

Looking at her keenly, Steve noted for the first time that there was something oriental about her. Perhaps it was the pallor of her cheeks; perhaps it was the long, narrow eyes of the deepest, glittering black. She could be Japanese. It was a fact not generally known to the public, that the natives of many of the northern islands of Japan—notably Nishino and Naka, and Sado Island in the Sea of Japan—were tall enough and clear enough of skin to pass for Filipinos and Javanese—and even as whites.

The woman mistook his sudden thoughtfulness for hesitation. Her lips parted sardonically. "Are you coming with me, Stephen Klaw?" she asked softly. "Or perhaps you are afraid? You think it's a trap?"

Klaw smiled tightly. "Afraid? Yes, let's call it that. I'm sorry. I don't believe a word of your story. I think it's a trap, and I'm not having any, thank you. Come on, baby. You're under arrest!"

A quick spasm passed across her face. It was hard to tell whether it was anger, fear, or merely surprise. But she made no resistance when he took her by the arm.

"You're making a mistake, Stephen Klaw. A terrible mistake—both for yourself and your country!"

KLAW GRINNED, and led her into the Department of Justice Building. Glancing behind, he saw that Kerrigan was covering their rear, just in case she should have had any companions. But when they reached the elevator, Kerrigan came in and joined them, nodding to Steve, in indication that no one was following.

Upstairs, in the temporary detention room, Steve turned the woman over to a matron.

"Charge her with suspicion of espionage," he instructed. "I'll be back in a little while to sign the complaint, and we'll arraign her at once!"

He and Johnny hurried up to the next floor, where the Director of the F.B.I. was waiting for them in the private office.

Swiftly, Steve told the Chief about the woman. "I haven't the faintest idea who she is, sir," he finished. "And I'm sure she won't talk. But I had to place her under arrest."

"Quite right, Steve," said the Director. "There's no doubt she's tied up with Oxenburg, of course." He stopped his impatient pacing, and stood facing Kerrigan and Klaw. His mouth was a thin, set line. "Sometimes I wish we could use the methods of the Gestapo! Imagine what the Gestapo would do to make prisoners talk—if they were convinced that there was a secret American army within Germany, ready to strike in five days! By the Lord Harry, they'd *make* their prisoners talk!"

Steve looked uncomfortable. "Well, sir, this woman must certainly know plenty. But I hardly think we could use a rubber hose on her, or stick burning toothpicks under her finger-nails."

There was a knock at the door, and in answer to the Chief's summons to enter, Dan Murdoch came in. He was carrying a manila envelope, and his darkly handsome face was wreathed in a smile of contentment.

"Got it!" he said.

The Director took the envelope from him swiftly. It had been sent through the mails, and was addressed: *Mr. Kurt Siglith, P.O. Box LT-13, General Post Office, New York, N.Y.*

"Come with me, you three!" said the Director. He led them through a side door, down a private corridor, to another room. This was a large conference room, with a huge map of the United States on one wall, and a detailed map of New York on the other.

In the center of the room there was a long conference table, at which were seated seven or eight men.

Kerrigan, Murdoch and Klaw stared as they saw the uniforms of some of those men. There were two generals, and a colonel of Army Intelligence, another colonel of the Army Air Force, and several men in civilian clothing. Kerrigan, Murdoch and Klaw recognized the two generals. They were staff officers, and it didn't seem possible that they had found time to come to New York on this matter.

The Director saw their looks of astonishment, and nodded. "Gentlemen," he said to the men at the table, "I want you to meet the three hellions who are called the Suicide Squad."

He did not introduce the men at the table, but just let it go at that, explaining swiftly to his three agents, "You can see the importance of the papers in this envelope. These gentlemen flew from Washington at my insistence, in the hope that we would be able to lay our hands on the Oxenburg Plan. Expecting that it would be in code, I insisted that the code experts from Army Intelligence come along!"

He laid the envelope on the table. "Gentlemen," he said, "here it is! The Oxenburg Plan!"

With a penknife he ripped the envelope open. While all the men watched breathlessly, he extracted a folded batch of onion-skin papers. He unfolded them, and spread them on the table. Every eye was focused on them. And a gasp of deep disappointment went up from one of the men in civilian clothes.

"That's the Formosa Code!" he explained. "It's just been

adopted by the Japanese! How is it that Oxenburg—a German—is using it?"

"I don't know," said the Director. "But whatever it is, you ought to be able to break it down, Mr. Fuller. You're the head of the Code Bureau."

He paused, seeing Fuller shake his head. "We've been working on the Formosa code for a month," he said. "As you see, it consists of Japanese ideographs—picture-words—arranged in a curious coded device. We've tried every possible combination of idea-words, but without success."

He began going through the sheaf of papers, examining each in turn, and shaking his head.

General Nichols, who was seated at the head of the table, picked up one of the sheets. "Look here, Fuller," the General said. "With these additional sheets to work from, you should be able to get further. I understand that there isn't a code in existence that can't be broken down, in time."

"Quite right," said Fuller. "And this code is no exception. Given time, we'll crack it. But I understand we have only five days."

He paused, then added reflectively, "There's a man somewhere in this country by the name of Nikander. He's half Asiatic, half European—the man who invented the Formosa Code. If we could find him—"

STEPHEN KLAW had been listening to this discussion, with the blood pulsing ever more swiftly through his veins. Suddenly he snapped his fingers, stood up.

"Excuse me, gentlemen!" he exclaimed. "Don't go away. I'll be back!" He motioned to Kerrigan and Klaw. "Let's go, Mopes!"

And before any of those at the conference table could hurl a question at them, the three G-Men were out of the room.

Neither Kerrigan nor Murdoch asked any questions of their partner. They merely followed him as he raced down the stairs to the floor below, where the detention room was located. They knew that if he didn't tell them what was in the wind, it was because there wasn't time; and they were content to follow his lead until he explained.

That was the way the Suicide Squad worked, and it was in part responsible for their success. If ever an outfit believed in teamwork, it was the Suicide Squad. Each of them had unlimited confidence and faith in the other two, and they were all ready to give unquestioning obedience to whichever of them was carrying the ball at the moment. In that way they had often been able to execute jobs requiring split-second timing, with brilliant success. People said their success was due to the fact that they were hair-brained fools who did not know the meaning of fear. But that was only partly true. Their success was mainly due to the fact that they operated like a well-integrated, well-greased piece of precision machinery—and trusted their lives to each other's judgment at all times.

Kerrigan and Murdoch waited in the outer room of the detention quarters, while Klaw went inside to the room with the barred windows where that strange and mysterious woman was being held. On the way in, Steve held a whispered consultation with the matron, who told him that the woman had been

126

searched, and her handbag taken from her. She showed him the handbag, which contained the usual personal articles that a woman carries, plus a small twenty-two calibre automatic. There were no identification papers of any kind in the bag. Apparently the woman had anticipated the possibility of being arrested.

"We just let her keep her cigarettes," the matron said. "She didn't make any fuss at all. Just said she thought you'd be back for her pretty soon."

"And here I am!" Klaw grunted. "Let me in there."

He entered the small room where the woman was confined, and found her smoking a cigarette, and standing near the barred window, looking out into the bleak afternoon drizzle. The rain was just beginning to change to hail, and Steve thought that it would be a hell of a Christmas in five days if they didn't succeed in breaking that Formosa Code.

The woman turned from the window and looked at him from under her long black lashes, and smiled slowly.

"Well?" she asked.

"All right," said Steve. "You win."

She dropped the cigarette on the floor, and stepped on it. "I suppose that means you've got hold of the Oxenburg Plans—but can't read them?"

"That's right. Our Code expert says it'll take a month to crack the code. We have to do it in five days."

"And you want me to tell you where to find the man who can read it?"

"Yes."

"You'll pay my price?"

"If it's within my power."

"All right. Release me. And come with me."

For a moment, Steve stood looking at her in exasperation. Then he shrugged. "Okay. You hold the cards."

He held the door open, and she swept out regally. In the ante-room, he got her purse from the matron and returned it to her, after extracting the automatic pistol and putting it in his own pocket. He grinned at her. "If this is a trap you're taking me into, *I'd* rather have the gun."

The woman didn't argue. "Let's hurry," she said. "The time is very short."

They went out into the corridor, and Steve made a surreptitious motion to Kerrigan and Murdoch.

In the street the woman said, "We don't need to take a cab. It's just around the corner."

Steve walked with her down the street to the corner. He glanced sideways at her, and saw that she was holding herself stiffly, as if under great strain. Somehow, he sensed that beneath that cold exterior, she was a bundle of nerves.

"Look here," he said. "Why don't you tell me your name? Have you any reason for keeping it a secret?"

"No," she said tonelessly. "I haven't any reason to keep it secret now that you've agreed to come with me." She paused. "My name," she said slowly, "is Anastasia Nikander!"

CHAPTER 4
A HALF-PINT OF DEATH—
DAILY

"NIKANDER!" EXCLAIMED Steve. "That's the name of the man who invented the Formosa Code!"

She nodded. "My husband!"

"Where is he? Here in New York?"

"No. He's three thousand miles away. That's why I told you time was so precious. It'll take time to reach him—and Baron Oxenburg will do everything in his power to prevent it!"

They had rounded the corner, and she stopped before the entrance of a small, shabby hotel. She threw swift, frightened glances around the street. "If Oxenburg's spies should see us," she whispered, "our lives wouldn't be worth a copper!"

She led the way into the lobby, among whose seedy occupants she looked oddly out of place.

Steve's forehead creased in a puzzled frown. "Why are you taking me in here? Why this mysterious—"

He broke off abruptly, for they had hardly taken half a dozen steps toward the elevator when two men moved over on either side of them. One thrust a gun into Steve's ribs, the other into Anastasia Nikander's.

They were men of small stature, dark and sour-looking. The one at the woman's side said, "Ah, Madame Nikander! So you have decided to go to the G-Men after all! And what is better, you have brought us one whom the Baron wants very badly. It was nice of you to bring Klaw to us!"

The woman uttered a faint gasp of dismay.

The man at Steve's left growled, "Do not move—"

But Klaw was already in motion. He had begun to swing around even before the other man had finished speaking, and his elbow swept the gun from his ribs. And at the same time, something very hard and very business-like descended upon the head of that man, in the shape of Johnny Kerrigan's clubbed revolver, while Dan Murdoch tackled the other one, reaching from behind for his gun arm, and, smashing a wicked blow down upon the fellow's head with his own revolver.

The whole thing took hardly more than five seconds, and the two men were going down under the assault from behind.

Grinning, Steve fumed and faced Kerrigan and Murdoch. "Nice work, Mopes," he said.

Anastasia Nikander stood gaping, still unable to comprehend the swift tide of deadly action which had gotten rid of their two captors so efficiently. The clerk came running over from the desk, and the elevator operator from his cage.

Johnny Kerrigan stood looking down ruefully at the two unconscious men. "Too bad we had to hit so hard," he said. "I bet they have fractured skulls, and won't be able to talk for days!"

"They couldn't tell you anything anyway," Anastasia Nikander said swiftly. "They are only the dregs of Oxenburg's army. They don't know where he hides."

Murdoch showed the clerk his F.B.I. identification. "We'll get these two bozoes out of here through the side door, so there won't be any fuss. We don't even have to report this. Oxenburg won't know what happened to his men, and he won't get a report of your bringing Klaw here, Madame Nikander."

Steve took her arm. "Let's be going," he said. "My partners will take care of everything."

There was a strange gleam of admiration in her eyes as she entered the elevator with Stephen Klaw.

"Do you know?" she said. "I'm beginning to have more and more respect for you Americans!"

"Thank you," said Steve. He gave her a puzzled look as she told the elevator operator to let them out at the ninth. "I can't figure what your game is," he told her frankly. "I don't know whether to count you as friend or enemy. That business in the lobby just now was certainly not a trap. You didn't know those eggs were waiting for you. But if you're a friend, why all this mysterious stuff?"

"You'll see!" she said cryptically.

They got off at the ninth floor, and Anastasia waited until the elevator door closed, and the cage had begun to descend. Then she said, "Come!"

She led him down the corridor, and when they passed Room 907, she nodded toward the door. "That's my room. But we're not going there."

Steve grimaced, but said nothing. The play was in her hands. At the end of the corridor, she opened the fire-door.

"We're going down to the eighth."

THEY DESCENDED the stairs to the eighth floor, and Steve followed her down the hall to the door of Room 807. This was directly beneath Anastasia Nikander's room, on the floor above. She glanced around furtively, as if fearful that there might be someone spying in the corridor, then when she was satisfied that there was no one, she dropped to one knee and fumbled under the carpet. In a moment she came up with a key, which she inserted in the lock. Before opening the door, she tapped a swift signal on the panel. Then she turned the key, and pushed the door open.

"It's all right, Ninovna darling," she said as she stepped into the room. "It's only I—Anastasia. I've brought the G-Man."

Steve followed her inside, and she immediately closed the door and locked it.

Steve hadn't known what to expect in this room. And now that he saw the nature of this secret which Anastasia Nikander had been so mysterious about, he was more puzzled than ever. For the thing which she had been at such pains to conceal was nothing more than a girl of about fifteen.

The girl had golden hair and blue eyes. She was lying on her back on the bed, with the blankets drawn up to her chin. Her head was turned sideways so that she could look at them, but otherwise she did not move. And Steve was shocked at the ghastly emaciation of that childish face. So thin was she that her eyes were like huge saucers by contrast; and there did not seem to be any blood in her at all.

She had been a beautiful girl, and she was still beautiful; but there was little life in her. She tried to raise her head, but it fell back weakly on the pillow. Her blue and bloodless lips moved with feeble effort, and she whispered, "You were away—so long, 'Stasia. I thought—you'd never come back…."

"Don't talk, darling," Anastasia said, with a sudden tenderness in her voice. "You must rest. I'll give you something."

She went to the night-table where there were some medicines and a carafe of water. She mixed a powder on a spoon with a few drops of water, and lifted the girl's head, and fed it to her.

"Sleep now, Ninovna dear," she whispered. "Everything will be all right."

Ninovna's lips moved feebly. Steve, who had stepped close to the bed, heard the words: "Don't let—that terrible Oxenburg… get me… again…."

And then the golden-haired girl's eyes closed, and she was asleep.

Anastasia lowered her head gently to the pillow and stood up and looked at Klaw.

"She's my sister," she murmured.

Steve raised his eyebrows. These two were so different—Ninovna golden-haired, fair-complexioned; Anastasia dark and lithe. But he didn't doubt Anastasia's word. He saw truth and sincerity now in her eyes, which were no longer veiled or secretive. He waited for her to explain. It mattered not at this moment that the fate of the country hung upon the deciphering of a coded paper; it mattered not that a dozen high officials sat at a table, wondering where he had gone. He saw the stark pain in Anastasia Nikander's eyes, and he waited upon her grief.

But she didn't keep him waiting long. She took a cigarette from her purse, and Steve held a light for her. She took a couple of quick, nervous puffs, and then began to speak in a low, tense voice.

"We are White Russians, Mr. Klaw; my husband, Nikolai Nikander, my sister Ninovna, and I. For twenty-five years our families have been outcasts, citizens of no country, entitled to the protection of no national or international law. My husband secured a position with the Intelligence service of one of the Balkan countries. He is a mathematician, and he worked out the Formosa Code. Then, when Germany overran the south of Europe, we came into their power. They—the Nazis—turned us over to Oxenburg, who arranged for us to come to this country. He forged passports for us, and brought us in through South America. We were entirely in his power, for at a word from him we could have been arrested by your immigration authorities."

"I see!" murmured Steve Klaw.

"There were many like us. There are many even now, who are forced to serve in the secret, vicious army which Oxenburg has formed here in America. Among others, there was Gregor Pavlov—and his sister, Lola."

Steve's eyes narrowed. "Pavlov! That's the name of the girl—" HE STOPPED short, remembering that no one was supposed to be aware that it was Lola Pavlov who had taken the bullet intended for Kurt Siglith. "It was this Gregor Pavlov who fired the shot at Kurt Siglith today, wasn't it?" he demanded.

She nodded. "Gregor Pavlov came to America with us, also as a tool of Oxenburg's. He's engaged to my sister Ninovna, here—he's madly in love with her. And through her, Oxenburg forced him to do things he hated. You must understand, Stephen Klaw, that none of us now want to see Germany win. Perhaps our fathers hated the Bolsheviks; but today, we know only that Russia is our mother country, and that she is in danger. We would help her if we could. But alas, we are in the toils of the Nazis."

"You mean that Oxenburg *forced* Gregor Pavlov to shoot Kurt Siglith?"

"Yes, yes. And then he forced him to commit suicide—to jump from that window rather than be captured alive!"

"But how could Oxenburg make him do a thing like that? Surely, this Gregor Pavlov could have refused? The worst that could have happened to him was that Oxenburg would denounce him to the immigration authorities, and he'd be arrested—"

Klaw stopped, seeing the strange and terrible smile upon her lips. "I will tell you how Oxenburg forced him to obey!" She stepped to the bed, and with a jerk drew away the covers from her sister's body.

"Look!"

Klaw uttered a gasp. The body of that poor golden-haired child, seen through the flimsy nightgown, was almost like that of a skeleton. Her arms were so thin and emaciated that they seemed to be mere arrangements of bones covered by a baggy film of skin. And upon her upper arms there were numerous punctures, such as might be made by a hypodermic needle.

"That is the work of The Ox!" Anastasia said fiercely. "His men seized Ninovna one night, and took her away to one of their many headquarters. They held her there. What could I do? I—her sister? What could Gregor do? Gregor—the man who loved her? We were both helpless. We could not complain to the police. Ninovna was here illegally, under a false passport. We dared do nothing."

She ground her cigarette out viciously in an ash tray, and hurried on. "Each day those fiends of The Ox took a half pint of blood from Ninovna's veins. Each day for a week. Then they let her rest for a week, and did it over again. Each day they sent the blood in a flask to Gregor. He had refused to do the bidding of Baron Oxenburg. But he could not hold out. He knew that those devils would drain every last drop of blood from the veins of the girl he loved. So he capitulated. He begged them only to spare Ninovna's life, and he would do whatever they asked."

"I see," Steve Klaw said quietly. "And they asked him to shoot Siglith?"

"Yes. Gregor was something of a marksman. He had won many medals and cups. So they used him for that. Oxenburg promised that he would release Ninovna if Gregor did only that one thing. He has kept his word, the fiend! He has released Ninovna—only to die. She has lost too much blood—"

"We'll fix that!" said Klaw. He went to the phone and jiggled the hook, then gave the operator the number of the F.B.I. Field Office.

"Send Doctor Glenn over here at once!" he ordered when he got his connection. Tell him to bring two or three blood donors. And arrange for day and night nurses. I want this patient given the best of care. The F.B.I. will foot the bill!"

He hung up and faced Anastasia Nikander. "All right. That's the best I can do. Your sister will live, if medical care can save her. And you needn't worry about deportation. Help us to break the Formosa Code before Christmas Day, and you'll all be made Honorary Citizens of the United States!"

THERE WERE tears in Anastasia Nikander's eyes—tears, unrestrained and unashamed. All her reserve, all her fearful repression, was broken down. She gently pulled the covers back over her sleeping sister, and then she turned and took Steve's hand and raised it to her lips.

He snatched his hand away. "Please—"

She smiled through her tears. "But now I must repay you—by helping you save your country—perhaps some day, *my* country!"

She lit another cigarette with shaking hands. "Listen carefully, Stephen Klaw. My husband, Nikolai Nikander, knows the Formosa Code by heart. If you will show him those papers, he will be able to read them off to you as if they were in his native language. You must get them to him at once—but—*he is in California!*"

"The address!" Steve demanded swiftly. "I'll phone the West Coast, and have him put on a fast Army Pursuit plane. We'll have relays at every Army Field across the country, waiting to carry him along. At three hundred miles an hour, he'll be here by tomorrow morning!"

She shook her head. "I'm sorry. It won't do. I can't give you my husband's address, for the simple reason that I don't know it."

"You don't *know* it?"

"All I know is, that Nikolai is in San Francisco. He was working for Oxenburg, naturally, under threat of what might happen to me and to Ninovna. He phones me by long distance, once each week, to make sure that I am still safe. Today, when he phoned me, I told him about Gregor and Ninovna, and he said that he would quit Oxenburg. He is through with him. He has gone into hiding somewhere in San Francisco, and even *I* do not know the address."

Steve Klaw felt a sudden empty feeling in the pit of his stomach. "But you said that you could put me in touch with him."

"Yes, yes. I can do that. But only in a certain way. Nikolai arranged it with me. I am to get to San Francisco somehow, after evading Oxenburg's spies. I am to go to a certain street corner, attired as an old woman, with a shawl about my head, a red shawl. I am to wait there for one hour, between seven and eight in the evening, each day, until he contacts me. He takes these precautions because he knows that Oxenburg will move heaven and earth to find him. By doing it this way, he will be able to watch that corner in San Francisco from some point of vantage, and he will know if I have been followed."

"I see," said Steve. "So in order to get in touch with Nikolai Nikander, I must take you to San Francisco."

"Yes—"

She was interrupted by the ringing of the telephone. Almost automatically she picked it up, and listened for a moment. Watching her, Klaw saw her already white face become even whiter. As if in a daze, she handed the phone to Steve Klaw. "It—it's *he*—The Ox! He wishes to talk with you!"

Steve's eyes became narrow. He took the instrument from her and spoke into it.

"Yes, Baron?" he said.

Oxenburg's smooth voice came through the receiver. "My

dear Klaw," he said suavely. "Do you imagine for a moment that you will ever be able to get Anastasia to San Francisco? Do you imagine that I will permit it?"

Klaw's hand tightened on the phone. "What makes you think I'm taking her to San Francisco?"

As he asked the question, he saw Anastasia Nikander put a hand to her mouth in sudden panic. She couldn't understand how Oxenburg knew she was going to San Francisco. She and Klaw had just made the arrangement a moment ago. Neither could Steve understand it.

At the other end of the wire, Oxenburg chuckled. "Nikolai Nikander will wait in vain for a woman with a red shawl. I assure you that Anastasia will never get there!"

"Ah!" said Stephen Klaw. "You know that, too?" His eyes darted around the room, searching for the dictograph which he was now sure must be somewhere in here. Only in that way could The Ox have acquired this information.

"You see, my friend," The Ox went on, "my plans for striking at America are complete, down to the last detail. Nothing shall be permitted to interfere with them; neither you nor your precious Suicide Squad, nor the whole United States Intelligence. On Christmas Day I strike!"

"Where?" asked Steve.

Oxenburg chuckled once more. "That, my friend, is something you will not know till *after* I have struck. The details are in those coded plans your experts are studying."

"Why are you making this phone call?" Steve demanded. "You

didn't call up just to make conversation with me. What do you want to find out?"

"Nothing, my friend. Nothing at all."

"Oh yes you do. You want to find out if we've cracked the code yet."

"I only want to warn you. It's useless for you to go to San Francisco in search of Nikolai Nikander. You'll never get there."

"Thank you for the warning," said Steve. "But—I'll be seeing you in 'Frisco!"

CHAPTER 5
DEATH RIDES THE SKY

TWENTY MINUTES later, Stephen Klaw was once more back in that conference room, with Anastasia Nikander. It took him only five minutes to explain to those men assembled there just what the situation was.

Almost before he had finished, General Nichols was on his feet. Now that there was something concrete to do, he demonstrated the speed and efficiency with which the Army could act.

"Be ready in fifteen minutes!" he said. "There'll be a fast Army bomber waiting for you at the field. Klaw, you and your two partners are going to take Mrs. Nikander to San Francisco, in that bomber. I'll give you an escort of fighter planes all across the country. You'll take these plans with you. It's up to you to get there and to find Nikolai Nikander. *You must not fail!*"

The bomber was already warmed up and ready to go when Kerrigan, Murdoch and Klaw arrived at the field with Anastasia

Nikander. Overhead, a squadron of three P-40s were circling, ready to fall in as escort.

Kerrigan had the coded papers in his pocket, and Anastasia Nikander walked between Klaw and Murdoch. They shook hands with the Director, and with General Nichols, who had accompanied them in another car, and then they climbed into the plane. Its interior had been stripped down of all excess equipment, in the interests of speed. Two benches had been installed behind the pilot and navigator, where the four passengers could sit. The door clanged shut, the O.K. came in over the radio, and the big plane got in motion. They took off easily, unburdened by the usual heavy load, and when they reached a thousand feet, the fighter planes fell in above them, at two thousand, ready to swoop the moment danger threatened.

"Well," said Johnny Kerrigan, "we're off. This looks like about the safest job we've ever been handed. With precautions like these, all we have to do is take a nap and wake up in 'Frisco!"

Dan Murdoch grunted. "If Oxenburg can stop us now, he's smarter than I give him credit for!"

But Anastasia Nikander was ill at ease. "I'm afraid," she whispered. "You don't know The Ox as I do. You don't know his resources. He'll stop us somehow!"

Up front, the pilot laughed. Over his shoulder he said, "I'd like to see anyone stop us! Those boys in the P-40s will mow down anything that comes near us—"

He broke off, with a sudden ejaculation of dismay, as something went zooming downward, past their plane. It was one of the P-40s, spinning wildly out of control. A split-second later, another of the pursuits came careening down, and barely a moment later, the third followed them. They caught a glimpse of the pilot of that third P-40 as it spun past them. He was slumped over the controls, held in the seat only by the safety belt.

"Good Lord!" exclaimed the navigator. "He's unconscious! He must have been doped or poisoned!"

Kerrigan, Murdoch and Klaw exchanged swift glances. Oxenburg was striking, all right, and striking fast. Some saboteur at the field must have doped the coffee which those pilots drank before taking off.

Peering downward, they saw the three pursuits crash, far below and behind them. One plane burst into flames down there on the ground, and the other two merely raised a cloud of dust. From up here it looked like a little bonfire where that first plane burned, but they knew it was the pilot's funeral pyre.

Their own pilot's face was white and set. "We've got to keep going!" he said. "Orders are to get through at any cost!"

Suddenly he uttered a cry of pain, and doubled over. "It's got—me—too—"

The big bomber went into a crazy spin as the pilot's hand froze on the stick, and the navigator made to reach for the controls, but he never got his hand on them, for he, too, clutched at his stomach with a groan.

The plane was spinning around in the air, completely out of control, and its nose headed downward, just like the P-40s. Anastasia and the three G-Men were hurled around inside, unable to keep their seats or their footing. With dreadful speed, the bomber hurtled crazily down toward the earth.

BLOOD, SWEAT AND BULLETS

IT WAS Dan Murdoch who managed to reach the pilot first. Both the pilot and the navigator were slumped down, either dead or unconscious. Murdoch kept his balance precariously as he struggled with the pilot's body, while the plane zoomed down to its doom. He wrestled the inert body out of the way, braced himself as best he could, and seized the controls.

For a terrible twenty seconds he fought the plane with all he had. Those twenty seconds were an eternity, until he brought it back out of the dead spin, just skimming the treetops. Then he slowly gained altitude.

Murdoch had been a Marine flyer before he had joined the F.B.I., and he had handled some pretty tricky crates on the China Station. He had been in some nasty spots in the air, but never anything like this. His face was white and set as he tried to keep the ship climbing.

Klaw took care of Anastasia, while Johnny Kerrigan came up forward and removed the bodies of the pilot and the navigator from their seats. Both men were dead.

"By God," Johnny said between clenched teeth, "I'd like to meet this Oxenburg in person!"

Murdoch was peering down at the terrain, trying to get his bearings. Far over to one side, they could still see the flames of the burning plane. The altimeter showed five thousand feet before Murdoch levelled off.

"I'll keep her high," he said, "in case we have to bail out. I've ridden as a passenger on this course, but I've never piloted it. I hate to admit it, guys, but I don't know if we're heading north, east, south or west!"

Stephen Klaw was caring for Anastasia, who had got a slight cut on the left cheek when she had been thrown violently around by the crazy acrobatics of the plane. He left her, and made his way forward to the navigator's seat, and donned the earphones.

"I'll contact Bolling Field, and ask them to give us a beam. We can ride right in on it then."

He spent ten minutes on the radio, and then gave up. Something was wrong with it.

"Not a spark of life in the damned thing!" he exclaimed. "Boy, our friend Oxenburg certainly is thorough!"

"Well," said Kerrigan, "there's still a half-hour of daylight. We can keep traveling till we recognize some landmark, or see an emergency field."

He had hardly said it, when something came crackling in like a stream of fire through the floor. It was like a fiery lance thrusting up from below.

"Tracer bullets!" exclaimed Klaw. Peering out, he saw a black plane without markings, zooming up past them. It had sneaked up on them from below, delivered its burst, and veered off.

"I'll be damned!" said Kerrigan.

The black plane swung around, went into a short, steep climb, and then came down at them in a dive, with twin machine-guns crackling from its wings, lancing streams of tracers straight at the bomber's nose.

Dan Murdoch said, "Boy! This is something we can put out teeth into!"

The bomber had been stripped down to the bone for speed, and it didn't even have machine guns. But Murdoch pulled the wheel back, and sent the big ship climbing straight up to meet the black plane in a head-on collision.

The two monsters of the air came at each other with devastating speed, the black plane's guns spouting slugs. Murdoch grimly held the course, his strong hands not moving on the controls once he had her lined up.

But the pilot of that black plane didn't have the guts. He pulled out sharply, trying to clear the bomber. Murdoch's teeth were set.

"Here goes!" he said. He pulled the wheel even farther back, gauging his distance with uncanny accuracy, and they heard the rumbling, clash of metal.

They were jarred around as by an earthquake, and for a moment it looked as if Murdoch had lost control. But he brought them back to an even keel, with most of the roof caved in, just as a great mass of flames swept down past them. The black fighter had caught fire!

They watched it spiral downward....

"Nice work, Dan," said Johnny Kerrigan. "That was the sweetest piece of flying I've ever seen!"

Anastasia Nikander sat with her hands clenched in her lap, her dark eyes a-glow with a queer light.

"I—I'm beginning to think we'll get there after all!" she whispered. "I—I think Baron Oxenburg should begin to be worried!"

Klaw grinned. "*Someone* has to do the worrying. It might as well be he!"

Johnny Kerrigan, who had been peering out at the terrain,

exclaimed, "There's Cleveland. I recognize it! Take her down, Dan. We'll patch up and re-fuel, and take off again!"

CHAPTER 6
YOU MUST NOT FAIL....

NOT FAR from the Oakland Ferry in San Francisco, there is a little restaurant and bar, which is frequented by men and women of a dozen nations. It is known as the Macedonian Grille, and it is run by a Greek refugee with an Armenian wife. To this place of an evening come Rumanians, Czechs, Russians and Syrians; Egyptians and Iraquis, Chinese and Netherlanders, fugitives from chaos.

There are many among them who have lost everything in their homelands, and who look forward to making this country their new home; there are others who are marking time here, doing what they can to help win the war, so they may some day return to their native hearths. Without guns, uniforms or glory, they're carrying on the war of humanity.

The Macedonian Grille is indeed a cosmopolitan spot, in atmosphere, language, and dress. The native costumes of a dozen countries are in evidence, and the idioms of a dozen languages fill the smoke-laden air.

It was, therefore, not strange to see a woman standing in the street before the place, garbed in gypsy costume, with a red shawl about her head. It aroused little comment, and few of those who passed vouchsafed her a second glance. People were busy with their errands, completing their Christmas shopping, carrying bundles the contents of which would go on their trees tomor-row; for this was Christmas eve.

For three nights now, they had seen this elderly appearing woman in her shawl, at the corner in front of the Macedonian Grille; and few of the passers-by were aware of the tumult of suspense and uncertainty which stormed within her breast.

The big, red-headed, broad-shouldered stevedore who lounged at the next corner knew what she was thinking; and the tall, dark-haired man sitting in the car across the street knew what she was thinking; and the slim young fellow sitting at the window table in the Macedonian Grille knew what she was thinking. For three days now, Kerrigan and Murdoch and Klaw had kept these vantage points each evening as Anastasia Nikander stood on the corner with her red shawl, awaiting the signal from her husband. And for three days now, the signal had not come. They had made their way across the continent from Cleveland in record time, had arrived with four days to spare before Christmas. But now there was nothing they could do except wait. Nikolai Nikander was the key to the preservation of America from that secret, planned attack by Baron Oxenburg's hidden army; without his interpretation of the Formosa Code, no preparation could be made to meet that attack.

Army Air Force bombers and fighters were ready at a hundred fields across the continent, waiting for word of the place where they must concentrate. Mobile units everywhere were on the alert for jumping-off orders. And all must wait upon that woman in the red shawl—

It was Stephen Klaw, seated at the window table of the Macedonian Grille, who first saw the limping man with the cane. He had passed, on the opposite side, twice in the last ten minutes, and he now made his limping way across the street. As he passed the woman in the red shawl he muttered something to her swiftly out of the corner of his mouth, and the woman started abruptly. Then she recovered herself, and in a moment she turned and followed the limping man with the cane.

At the same time, Stephen Klaw got up from his table and paid his bill, and went out; Johnny Kerrigan threw away his cigarette and began to amble idly down the street; and Dan Murdoch got the car started, turned it around, and slowly paced the limping man.

ALL THREE of them were taut and ready for anything, because the limping man might not be from Nikolai Nikander at all; he might be an emissary of Baron Oxenburg, sent to trap Anastasia. They knew very well that Oxenburg, after failing to knock them down out of the sky, was moving heaven and earth here in San Francisco, to locate the spot at which Anastasia was to meet her husband. That was the one thing which Oxenburg did not know. There was no doubt that he had agents out everywhere in the streets of the city, with orders to look for a woman in a red shawl. He might have discovered her here—might have sent an agent to lead her and the Suicide Squad into a death trap.

The limping man turned into a dark alley, and Anastasia hesitated a moment, while Kerrigan and Murdoch and Klaw closed up on her. Then, with her chin up, she stepped into the alley.

The limping man was waiting there for her. He flung away his cane, and threw his arms about her. " 'Stasia! I was in Oakland until tonight. I could not come sooner. Oxenburg's men have been combing the city for me! My darling, how glad I am to see you safe!"

"Nikolai!" she exclaimed. "I did not recognize you! You are disguised!"

"And with reason!" he said bitterly. "My life hangs by a hair—"

He paused suddenly, his body tautening, and his arms coming away from around his wife, as he saw the three shadowy figures of Kerrigan, Murdoch and Klaw slipping into the alley. "We are betrayed—"

"No, no, darling!" she exclaimed. "These three are friends!"

It took several moments of swift explanation to convince Nikolai Nikander that he had nothing to fear from these three. Then they rushed him and Anastasia into the car, and Murdoch drove at breakneck speed across the bridge to Oakland. They hustled him up the back way into the Oakland Field Office of the F.B.I., and into a private room with armed guards in the corridor. There, Kerrigan spread the coded plans before him.

Nikander's eyes widened.

"Can you read them?" Murdoch demanded.

Nikander smiled. "As easily as English or Russian. This is the Formosa Code—"

There were two expert F.B.I. shorthand stenographers present with pencils poised over notebooks, and a dictaphone machine to take it down on records in addition. Nikander began to read, his voice tightening.

The preparations for that blow to be struck on Christmas day were complete and terrible. At San Diego and three other Naval

Bases; at two Navy Yards; at an ammunition dump in Jersey and at the drydocks in Newport News, there were striking forces of shock troops assembled in secret hiding places with gas bombs ready for the first assault, to be followed by demolition squads which would use high explosive to wipe out the plants and installations completely. At midnight on Christmas Eve they were to strike; and the result would be to leave America's war potential crippled for many months to come—enough time to give the Axis a breathing-spell and consolidate its positions in Europe and the Far East.

As Nikander read these papers, Kerrigan, Murdoch and Klaw were on phones to Washington, New York and San Diego, holding the lines open; and each stenographer in turn would get up, go to a microphone hooked into all those open lines, and read back his notes.

All that night, from Washington, orders crackled over the ether, setting in motion the Armed Forces of the United States to frustrate this attack from within.

And as the evening wore on, the raids came off—one here, one there, in widely separated spots across the continent. The dragnet brought in sulky, sullen Nazis, Japs, shock troops of villainy rendered impotent by the surprise raids. And when, by midnight, the last of those raids was completed and the hastily prepared concentration camps full of prisoners, Nikolai Nikander was conducted to a hotel with his wife, where they were given a suite of rooms, protected by F.B.I. guards.

And Kerrigan, Murdoch and Klaw grinned at each other and shook hands. But at once, Steve Klaw's face became grave.

"There's one thing we've failed in, Mopes," he said.

And neither Kerrigan nor Murdoch needed an explanation of what he meant. The one man who had not showed up in that dragnet was Baron Oxenburg.

"The Ox is still on the loose," said Murdoch. "We'll be hearing from him."

"Let's go out and have a drink," said Johnny Kerrigan. "We'll drink to the next time we meet Baron Oxenburg."

"Let's hope," Steve Klaw said piously, "that he stays healthy—till we meet him!"

THE SUICIDE SQUAD AND
THE TWINS OF DEATH!

CHAPTER 1
THE DOOR OF DEATH

THE DOOR opened a bare twelve inches, allowing a mixed odor of garlic, *tequila*, stale cigarette smoke and perspiration to waft out into the dark alley. A Mexican in a checkered jacket and a broad-brimmed hat thrust his head out and said, *"Ps–st!"*

Stephen Klaw, feeling his way along the smelly alley, stopped short. His hands were dug deep in his coat pockets.

A rat scurried away somewhere in the darkness, making a slimy, slithering sound. Not far away, a church bell was tolling the midnight hour; while high in the sky a patrol plane's motors whined their defiance of the black and moonless heavens. But here in the alley there was no other sign of life than the scurrying rat and the Mexican's sibilant whisper.

There was the dull glint of metal in the Mexican's hand. He was holding a gun close to his side as he peered into the darkness, trying to discern the figure of Stephen Klaw.

Klaw had become motionless against the grimy wall, almost directly opposite the doorway. He waited just a second or two, and then he said softly, *"Aqui."*

The Mexican jumped as if he had been shot.

They appeared like a pair of grim, avenging gods from another world....

Klaw chuckled. Then he spoke very low, in English. "Is this where Enrico Morales lives?"

The Mexican hesitated. Then he said, "Excuse, Señor, please. Will you permit that I look at your face? A flashlight for a moment, no?"

"For a moment, yes," Klaw replied. "But put that gun away first. It would be too bad if you tried to use it. I've got you covered."

"But yes, Señor. Indeed, yes!" The Mexican very carefully slipped the gun into a pocket of his tight-fitting trousers.

Klaw took his left hand from his coat pocket, produced a small pencil flashlight from an inner pocket, and directed a subdued beam of light upward into his own face for a fraction of a minute. Then he clicked the light off.

"Ah!" said the Mexican. "A thousand pardons, Señor. But you comprehend that great caution is required in this transaction."

"Sure," said Steve.

"And now, if it pleases the Señor to give the password?"

"Busco unas ratas," said Klaw. "I seek rats."

"Bueno!" said the Mexican. He flung the door wide open, and moved to one side. "Enter, Señor!"

Stephen Klaw took a single step forward. And then he saw the trap into which he was walking.

There was just a dim light within the room, hardly enough to distinguish objects very clearly. They were counting, no doubt, on his eyes being momentarily blinded by the change from pitch darkness to light. But Klaw needed only to glimpse the vague shape of the machine-gun on the tripod at the far side of the room, and the woman bending over it, with her hand on the trip, and a Mexican beside her, holding the long, snaking cartridge belt.

STEPHEN KLAW'S reactions were the instinctive reflexes of the seasoned fighting man. He flung himself to one side of the open doorway as the machine-gun burst into wicked, chattering life. Tracer bullets smashed into the opposite wall of the alley. Plaster chipped, and hot lead ricochetted. For thirty seconds, the alley was filled with the deadly, staccato orchestration. Then the chatter ceased as suddenly as it had begun. The tracer bullets must have shown the woman at the machine-gun that she had missed. The dancing thunder echoed up and down the alley, and then there was silence.

The church bell had ceased to toll. The powerful whine of the patrol plane was gone. Even the rat had scampered off.

In the darkness of the alley, Klaw rested on one knee, close beside the doorway. Both automatics were in his hands now. He made no sound. His breathing was noiseless. He did not move.

Inside the house, no one moved either. The light had been doused by some one in there.

Time ticked away. There was no sound or hint of movement, within or without. It was a contest of nerves.

And then, faintly, a foot scraped in the alley—behind Stephen Klaw! Some one had stolen out from the other side of the house, and had crept around to the mouth of the alley.

Whoever was there must have realized that he had given himself away, for almost immediately, a revolver began to blast. Orange flashes of flame stabbed the darkness, and bullets screamed.

But Klaw, too, had begun to shoot, whirling and firing simultaneously with the scraping sound of that foot in the alley. He used both guns, bracketing the orange flashes, then swinging the muzzles together to center upon the spot where he knew the killer stood. He rose to his full height as he fired, hugging the wall with his back, disdainful for the moment of possible attack from the open doorway behind him.

It was a deadly duel in the dark, and it ended as abruptly as it had begun. A scream sounded at the mouth of the alley, high above the blasting thunder of the gunfire, and the orange flashes ceased. The slugs stopped their screech. Klaw made out the figure of a man falling forward. He stopped shooting. Instinctively, he had counted his shots. It was important, in a battle, to know how many cartridges remained. He knew that he had three left in each automatic. Six shots with which to tackle the machine-gun which was still inside there, pointing at the open doorway.

He stood quite still, with his back to the wall, both guns ready. The dead man at the mouth of the alley did not move. Neither did Steve.

AFTER A moment, there was a faint slither of movement from within the house. *"Pedro!"* a woman's voice called softly. *"Es muerte el Americana!"* Her voice was remarkably soft, hardly the voice of a woman who had just tried to cut a man down in cold blood with a machine-gun. But the question she had asked in Spanish was bloodthirsty enough.

Still hugging the wall, Steve muffled his voice and said, *"Si. Es muerte."*

"Bien acabado!"—Well done!—she exclaimed, and came hurrying out, clicking on a flashlight.

Stephen Klaw placed the muzzle of his gun against her ribs. "Hold still, sister."

She stopped stock still, and a gasp escaped her lips. Her face showed white in the darkness, and her eyes glittered. It was impossible to tell if she was young or old, beautiful or ugly. But there was a faint and mysterious aroma of perfume about her, almost exotic in its flavor; and her body was long and slim.

"You—you said the American was dead!" she whispered, in English.

Klaw chuckled. "Maybe I exaggerated a little. I'm not quite dead. But Pedro is. Too bad."

He reached over and took the flashlight out of her unresisting hand, and turned its beam up into her face—and sucked in his breath, sharply! The flashlight revealed a face of almost unbelievable beauty. Great coils of black hair lay piled upon her head. Her eyes were dark, deep pools of mystery, as black as her hair. She wore a black lace *mantilla* which set like ebony against the flawless whiteness of her curving throat.

"How could anyone as beautiful as you be so bloodthirsty?"

She stood straight and unmoving, with the muzzle of the gun against her ribs. Her eyes flashed with a strange, hard light of hatred as her gaze locked with Klaw's in the dark.

" 'Bloodthirsty?'" she repeated huskily. "You do not know how I hate you. One death is not enough for you. If I could, I would kill you a dozen times over!"

Steve looked puzzled. "Why do you hate me like that? We've never met before, have we?"

Her lips curled scornfully. "But we shall meet again!" Then she deliberately turned her back on him. "Shoot me. Let us see how well you make war on women!" Then she bent low, and began to run lithely down the alley, away from the open doorway.

Klaw's face was grim. His finger was curled around the trigger of his automatic. But he couldn't bring himself to shoot. In that single moment, the woman's slender, black-clad figure merged with the night and disappeared into it; and she was gone—almost soundlessly.

Klaw smiled wryly in the dark. He didn't attempt to pursue her. It would have been useless. Besides he was already swinging the beam of the flashlight into the house. He remembered having seen a second Mexican, feeding the belt into the machine gun. One of them lay dead in the alley. Was the other still in there?

OUTSIDE, THERE were sounds of men shouting, and women babbling. Some one was blowing a whistle. The denizens of all the surrounding alleys were calling back and forth, asking each other what was happening, hazarding wild guesses as to the cause of the shooting. But it was significant that no one came into the alley, no other door opened. These people knew better than to poke their noses into violence and death in these days of wartime espionage. Here in this sleepy little Mexican town five miles below the border, they had seen much of intrigue and mystery—and death in the last couple of years. And they were frightened.

But the shrill whistle that sounded not far off was a different matter. That was the whistle of the *policia*. Soon they would be here, the Mexican police. Before they arrived, Stephen Klaw had to finish the job he had come to do.

Reckless now of the chance that the second Mexican might be lying in wait for him, he sprang into the room.

A curtain jerked spasmodically, and a gun barked behind it. A slug tore through its folds and whistled close to Steve's ear. Klaw dove for the curtain and tore it aside, keeping his automatic thrust forward, his finger curled around the trigger. He yanked hard, and the curtain ripped at the top and came tumbling down upon the head of the man behind it. The man squealed like a frightened rat, and Steve smashed the barrel of his automatic down on his head. He hit hard, in order to overcome the cushioning afforded by the swirling curtain. The man buckled at the knees, and went down.

Steve had dropped the flashlight in order to yank the curtain. It lay on the floor, its fall softened by the resilient casing around it, and its light lanced along the boards. He snatched it up again, and stepped over the motionless figure of the Mexican, still entangled in the heavy drapery. He entered the second room, and glanced swiftly around.

In the rear wall of this inner room, there was an open window, testifying with mute eloquence of the method of Pedro in stealing out for his unsuccessful flanking attack. But it was not upon this that Steve's gaze lingered. He stared at the cot over at the left, on which lay a man. The other was trussed up with dozens of thick strands of rattan-rope. Half a dozen twisted strands of the rope were tied into his mouth as a gag, cutting cruelly into the corners of his lips.

He was old and emaciated, this bound prisoner. His hair was white and his skin wrinkled, and the blue veins stood out like cords in his bound and straining forearms. Blue, pain-wracked eyes peered up into Klaw's flashlight. He wore only a pair of torn and faded trousers, otherwise he was naked to the waist; and his skin was cut and bruised by blows, and seared with fire.

A cold pulse of anger stirred within Stephen Klaw as he saw the torture to which the old man had been subjected. He stepped to the side of the cot, laid down the flashlight and the automatic, and proceeded with swift fingers to undo the gag between the old man's teeth.

"Take it easy, Mr. Morales," he said. "I'll have you out of this in a minute—"

HE GOT the gag off, and started on the rattan ropes which bound Morales' arms at his sides. The old man had been watching with eyes that shone wide and urgent in the bright flashlight. He moved his stiff jaw sideways as if to limber it, and then he spoke with painful haste, each word costing him an effort which seemed to cut through him like a knife. His breath came in tortured gasps.

"Do not bother, Señor Klaw—do not bother—with the other—ropes. It is of no use. I will be dead—before I am free of them. Listen carefully. I should be dead now, but I have forced myself to remain alive—hoping that you would come in time...."

He paused, gathering strength.

Klaw's eyes softened. He placed a hand gently under the old man's head. "Go on, Mr. Morales," he said. There was a deep and reverent respect in his voice; for Stephen Klaw saw and recognized the fighting heart within the breast of old Enrico Morales.

"Listen to me carefully," the old man gasped. "The name of the man you seek who holds a knife to the throat of your country—and of mine—who knows what it was before; but now, he is known only as Blond Otto."

"Ah!" said Stephen Klaw. His eyes flickered. The name on the old man's lips stirred a restless chord of memory within his mind. "I think I know the one you mean. Blond Otto the Hangman!"

"That is the one!" Morales gasped eagerly. "Since the last war he has lived in Mexico, posing as an American oil man. He speaks English as well as you; he has built slowly and carefully for this day. He has an army of agents, money, arms, everything. He will strike somewhere soon. You—must—stop him…."

Morales' voice trailed away, and his eyes began to close. Klaw supported him with one arm, his whole attention centered on the old man. At that moment, if those who had tried for his life before had returned, Klaw might have been easy prey. He bent close. "What about Otto the Hangman?" he demanded. "What is he planning?"

Morales' eyes flickered open. He was barely conscious. But that iron will of his kept him alive for yet another moment. "You must go to New York. There is one there by the name of Skopa—a little man with a little soul, who has taken the gold of Blond Otto. Skopa will talk. He does not know much—but enough to… perhaps help you…."

Once more. Morales' voice died away almost to a whisper.

Klaw bent closer. "How will I find this Skopa?" he demanded.

"Telephone… Quincy 2-4142…."

A dreadful spasm of pain took possession of the old man's body. His neck arched high, the veins standing out in his temples like ugly cords; then he uttered a tortured gasp, and went limp.

Very slowly, Stephen Klaw laid him back on the cot. He got to his feet, picking up the gun and the flashlight. His lips became tight as he looked down upon the face of the dead man. Morales had kept himself alive by a sheer, brave effort of will—until he had passed on the word which would transfer his burden to the younger shoulders of Stephen Klaw… and it was as much due to his indomitable courage as to Steve's own efforts that the F.B.I. now had the information it wanted.

CHAPTER 2
THE BARGAIN

THE INJURED Mexican was stirring once more, his head encased in the folds of the curtain. Steve's eyes smoldered as he stepped up to the squirming figure and pulled the drape off the fellow's head. He lit the oil lamp on the table.

The man looked up at him with bleary eyes, and touched the back of his head. "What's your name, bud?" Steve asked him.

"Miguel."

"Who was the woman?"

"What woman?"

"Come out of it," Steve said. "You know whom I mean."

The Mexican's eyes veiled. "I know of no woman."

Steve grunted. "How would you like to take a bullet in the guts, my friend?" He jerked his head toward the still figure of Señor Morales, on the cot. "After seeing him, I'd cheerfully give it to you."

The man leered up at him. "You *Americanos* do not kill in cold blood."

Klaw's eyes narrowed. "Better watch that accent—you're no Mexican."

"Go to the devil!" the other said.

Klaw kept the light in his eyes. He smiled tightly. "You're a German spy. I'll turn you over to the Mexican police. Mexico is at war with Germany. You know what that means, don't you? It means the gallows!"

The fellow raised himself up on one elbow. "Go to the devil!" he repeated. "Let the *policia* come. I do not fear them."

Klaw looked quizzically at him. There was something wrong here. He could see in the other's eyes that he was not one to face death bravely, or stoically. And yet—he was not afraid of the consequences of arrest by the Mexican police.

The heavy tread of the *policia* was close by, now. Steve heard them swing into the alley. He shrugged resignedly. "I hoped you'd talk," he said. "Now it's too late."

The other merely leered up into the light. *"We shall see for whom it is too late!"* he whispered malevolently.

A moment later, the police swept into the shack.

There were half a dozen of them, natty in their blue uniforms, and wearing the new steel helmets which had been issued by the governor of the province. Each had a short carbine in his hand, and the sergeant had a powerful electric torch which he flashed into the room, bathing both Stephen Klaw and the prostrate man in its blinding light.

Steve had pocketed his gun. "United States Federal Bureau of Investigation," he said to the sergeant, showing his wallet. "I am here by special permission of His Excellency, the Governor of the Province. Here is the letter of authority issued by him. I ask you to arrest this man, who is a German spy."

"But certainly, Señor," said the sergeant. He made a motion with his hand to his men, and they spread out in a circle, around Steve, leveling their carbines.

STEVE BLINKED. He glanced around. He was surrounded by a circle of threatening muzzles, all pointing at himself. He turned and looked into the light which the sergeant held. "Look here, Sergeant, you don't understand—"

"I understand well enough," the sergeant barked. "Be still!" He went over and bent beside the injured man, and helped him to his feet. "You are all right, Hedrik?" he asked, switching from Spanish to German.

"Yes, I'm all right, Ritter," the other replied, also in German, "merely a bad knock on the head. This one—" jerking a thumb at Klaw "fights like the very devil. He killed Hans in the alley."

"Yes, I saw," said the sergeant, whom Hedrik had addressed as Ritter. "But what about Carola? What happened to her?"

"This one got her at the point of a gun, but she escaped. Leave it to Carola. She's clever!"

The sergeant grunted, and turned to Steve. "Herr Klaw, you know of course, that you are about to die?"

Steve scowled. "Just let me get this straight before I kick off. Your name is Ritter?"

The sergeant bowed, in precise military fashion, from the hips. "Captain Ritter von Reichenthal, at your service. It was a simple matter to arrange this meeting. My men and I overpowered the police patrol, and took their places. We did so, in order that any disturbance which might arise here when you arrived would never be reported to the *jefe*."

166

"I see!" Klaw said grimly. "And we thought that the reports of the efficiency of the German spy system south of the border were exaggerated!" He looked around at the ring of steel which encircled him, and smiled bitterly. His gaze sought the bogus sergeant of *policia* once more. "What about that woman—Carola? Who is she?"

A strange and secretive look came into the eyes of Captain Ritter von Reichenthal. "We will not speak of her!" he said shortly.

"Not even to one who is about to die?"

Von Reichenthal waved impatiently. He uttered a word of guttural command to his men, and they swung out of the circle, into a line. Their carbines, cocked, centered upon Stephen Klaw, fingers on triggers, ready for the order to fire. And then Ritter von Reichenthal was watching him, narrow-eyed and calculating. "You are a brave man, Herr Klaw?"

"What's eating you?" Steve wanted to know.

THE GERMAN shrugged. "Even a brave man does not wish to die uselessly, like a rat in a vermin-infested alley in a cheap Mexican town."

Steve smiled. "What would you know about what a brave man wishes?"

Von Reichenthal flushed. "I pass by your insult. I can afford to overlook it. I will state my proposition. You, *Herr* Klaw, are a member of the so-called Suicide Squad, not so?"

Steve was silent.

"You have two partners—Kerrigan and Murdoch."

"Well?"

Von Reichenthal's eyes were glowing with eagerness. "You may buy your life, *Herr* Klaw, in exchange for theirs. Kerrigan and Murdoch are in Mexico—perhaps not far from here, waiting for word from you. We, of the German Secret Service, know that much. Tell us where they are, and you may walk out of here a free man!"

Steve grinned at him.

Von Reichenthal's mouth thinned to a grim line. "You please to jest with me, eh? Very well. Prepare to die, *Herr* Klaw. Kneel!"

"I'll take it standing up," Stephen Klaw said.

Every muscle of his body was taut as a bowstring, his brain keen and quick and alive, and ready for last-minute action. In his pockets were two automatics....

There was no chance, of course, of his coming out of this alive. The odds were too great, even considering the element of surprise. There were six of the soldiers with carbines, besides von Reichenthal with a heavy Luger in his hand. Hedrik had picked up his revolver from the floor. Eight against one. Klaw would take some of them with him, certainly. But he knew well enough that this was the end.

He had often pictured to himself the end when it would finally come—and this was inescapably it. Fighting against odds was the task of the F.B.I.'s Suicide Squad, by definition. Only one thing was lacking, and that was the presence of Johnny Kerrigan and Dan Murdoch.

Originally, there had been a total of five in the Suicide Squad. Then one day there had been a job from which only four returned. Then there were only three.

Tonight, as Stephen Klaw stood facing those carbines, he knew that tomorrow there would be only two—and maybe the next day one—or none.

Von Reichenthal bit his lip in vexation. Steve knew well enough that the German had not expected him to talk, to betray his partners. But the captain might have entertained a faint hope that Klaw would weaken at the last moment, would in some way try to bargain for his life. He was disappointed, and angry. He raised a hand to his troop.

"Ready!" he barked. "Aim...."

CHAPTER 3
TWIN TO MADNESS

THAT WAS the last word which the Herr Captain Ritter von Reichenthal ever spoke upon this earth. His voice was drowned out by the sudden blasting thunder of smashing gunfire from the direction of the doorway. Like a pair of grim, avenging gods from another world, two tall men had suddenly appeared there out of the night which shrouded the alley, each with a pair of heavy revolvers. Shoulder to shoulder they stood there, guns blasting, grinning, yet never moving.

Dan Murdoch, tall and dark-haired and dark-eyed, handsome and debonair; Johnny Kerrigan, red-haired and powerfully built, with the shoulders of a stevedore and the forearms of Vulcan; these were the partners of Stephen Klaw—the other two-thirds of the Suicide Squad.

Where one goes, the other two are not far away! That was the slogan of the Suicide Squad—Von Reichenthal may have known it. Now he was learning just how true it was, but the lesson would be of no value to him. Von Reichenthal was dead before the driving slugs had smashed his body back across the room, into the wall.

At the same moment that Kerrigan and Murdoch had begun to shoot, Stephen Klaw's two automatics came out of his pockets, spitting death with swift peppery barks. The rain of lead smashed into the soldiers with their carbines, and the room thundered, and the walls trembled, and death laughed high and loud above the storm of gunfire.

The fusillade from the guns of the Suicide Squad lasted barely seconds; but when the thunder ceased, not a man of the troop remained on his feet. Three or four were wounded, the others dead—including Hedrik.

Kerrigan and Murdoch stepped into the room, across the shambles, and grinned at Stephen Klaw.

He grinned back at them. "Hi, Mopes," he said.

Johnny Kerrigan winked at Dan Murdoch. "It's a good thing we got here, Shrimp," he said to Steve. "Another minute, and we'd have had to bring flowers!"

Dan Murdoch's eyes were twinkling. "My, my," he said. "It's getting so, we hate to let you go out by yourself at night. How did you make out? What's our score?"

"I saw Morales," Klaw gestured. "Come over here," he said quietly. "Take a look." He showed them the tortured and emaciated body upon the cot in the inner room.

"Morales!" exclaimed Murdoch.

"Damn them!" growled Johnny Kerrigan. "Look what they did to him!"

DAN MURDOCH swallowed hard. "Anyway, we paid off for him. Wherever he is now, Enrico Morales will know that we evened the score. We got every damned one of them!"

"Not every one," Steve said slowly. "I'm afraid I let the worst one get away—a woman."

"A woman?" Johnny repeated.

"She's the most beautiful thing this side of hell—and the most dangerous. You ought to see her handle a machine-gun!" He jerked his thumb toward the tripod, which was lying on its side on the floor. "And she really hates our guts!"

"Who is she?" Johnny demanded.

"All I know is that her name is Carola. And something tells me we'll run into her again. If we do, don't let her beauty fool you."

Several of the wounded men were groaning with pain, trying to extricate themselves from the welter of bodies on the floor. Outside, men and women were shouting once more. This time, the neighborhood seemed to be fully aroused. Running feet were pounding out in the alley, and whistles were blowing.

"Let's get out of here," Steve said suddenly. "Morales lived long enough to give us a lead. We don't want to stay and explain to the Mexican police."

"Okay," said Kerrigan. "Let's be going!" He doused the kerosene lamp, and plunged the room in darkness. They felt their way to the window in the rear, and climbed out, one at a time. They hurried down to the mouth of this rear alley, swung left into another one, and soon lost themselves in the night. All about them, the town seemed to have been electrified into life. Dark shapes flitted past them, and men threw swift questions to them in hurried Spanish, which they answered in the same language. In a few minutes they reached the Plaza, and Kerrigan led the way to a little side street where they had left their car. Five minutes later, big Johnny was tooling the auto north along the Pan American Highway toward the United States border.

"Remember this number, Mopes," Stephen Klaw said. "Quincy 2-4142. It's the key to Blond Otto! According to Morales, Blond Otto is in New York. And a little rat by the name of Skopa is the one we need to contact."

"Skopa!" exclaimed Johnny Kerrigan, whose memory was encyclopedic. "That must be Armand Skopa. Hungarian. Did little espionage jobs for the Hungarian consulate up to the time of Pearl Harbor, and then dropped out of sight. He's wanted for murder of a waitress in one of those Hungarian dives on Fourteenth Street. He's a vicious little beggar. His specialty is the knife. Always in the back."

"Hm," Dan Murdoch said dreamily. "Sounds like an unpleasant character. Personally, I'd rather meet Steve's mysterious woman. She intrigues me—"

Dan Murdoch broke off abruptly as Johnny Kerrigan slammed on the brakes and the car screeched to a halt. In the road ahead, limned in the headlights, they had glimpsed the figure of a woman, with thumb upraised to hitch a ride. The car slid past her about fifty feet, and looking through the rear window, they saw her running to come up to them.

"Well, I'll be damned!" said Stephen Klaw.

Murdoch, seated beside him in the rear, looked at him questioningly.

Klaw grinned. "Speak of the devil!" he said.

Murdoch's eyes widened. "You mean—"

"I mean that you've got your chance to meet our mystery baby. There she is, boys—believe it or not!"

DAN MURDOCH whistled through his teeth. He was about to say something, when the woman came abreast of the car. She was no longer wearing the black mantilla about her shoulders, but she was as beautiful as ever. Her face was flushed, as if from excitement or exertion, and she was breathing fast.

"Excuse me," she said, peering into the driver's seat at Johnny Kerrigan. "I'm an American. I—wonder if you'd give me a lift to the border. I was coming home from Tia Juana, and my car broke down."

"Why sure," Johnny Kerrigan said. "It'll be a pleasure to take you to the border. Hop right in!"

The woman went around to the other side, and Johnny reached over and threw open the door. She climbed in, cast only a quick glance at Klaw and Murdoch, and seated herself. Johnny started the car at once.

In the rear, Stephen Klaw watched the woman's back, with a sardonic smile on his lips. It was the height of irony that this woman, whom he had allowed to escape once, should thus have delivered herself into their hands. True, they could not make an arrest on Mexican territory. But now that they had her in the car, they could keep her in it until they crossed the border.

Steve leaned forward, and tapped her on the shoulder. "Hello," he said.

The woman turned around, and looked him full in the face. He saw now that she was much younger than he had thought she was. Her black hair was disarranged, no longer coiled high on her head, but hanging loose, as if it had come undone from strenuous exertion of some kind. But her eyes as she turned to look at Steve were just as black, and their meaning as deeply hidden as it had been when she had faced him in the alley.

Steve watched her like a hawk, waiting for the start of surprise which should be coming when she recognized him. But he was disappointed. No flicker of recognition showed in her face, no gasp of alarm came from her lips. Instead, she merely nodded and said, "Hello."

Steve blinked. She was indeed a marvelous actress, this mysterious Carola. And she must have supreme control of herself, to have avoided making some betraying gesture.

"This is Mr. Murdoch," Steve said pleasantly. "And the big red-headed hairy ape at your side is Johnny Kerrigan." He paused, then added drily, "As for me, I guess I don't need to introduce myself. You and I have already met."

THE WOMAN nodded to Murdoch, smiled at Kerrigan, and then turned a puzzled glance upon Steve. "You say we've met before? I don't recall it. My name is Anita Zogchinski." She smiled, with just the right touch of embarrassment. "I suppose I should say, Countess Zogchinski. You see, I've only been married a week. I married Count Ladislas Zogchinski, a Polish nobleman. He came here right after the blitzkrieg in Poland. He was wounded in the siege of Warsaw, and hasn't been able to go back to fight for his country as yet—"

"Sure, sure," said Steve. "And will you tell us if it was this Count Zogchinski who taught you how to use a machine gun?"

She turned all the way around, and looked squarely at Steve. "I'm sorry, Mr. Klaw, but I really don't know what you're talking about—"

"Naturally not," Steve said suavely. "I suppose you never heard of such a thing as a machine gun—or of Enrico Morales, or of Captain Ritter von Reichenthal!"

"Why no, I don't think I have—"

Johnny Kerrigan was slowing up as they reached the Mexican customs shed at the border. The Mexican guard nodded to them to pass on, without even making a cursory examination of their car, when Johnny showed the special F.B.I. pass, countersigned by the President of the United States. At the American gate they had no trouble either, and in a moment they were rolling along on United States soil.

Stephen Klaw took a deep breath. "All right, Countess Anita Zogchinski, alias Carola!" he said. "I arrest you in the name of the Government of the United States of America, on a charge of espionage. If it turns out that you're telling the truth about being a native American, the charge will be amended to treason!"

"Treason!" she exclaimed. "There—there must be some mistake. You—you called me Carola. That's my sister's name."

Steve's eyes twinkled. "I suppose you're going to tell us now that you have a twin sister named Carola?"

"Exactly. Carola Corbey is my twin sister. I was Anita Corbey before I was married."

"Tut, tut, Lady," said Dan Murdoch. "Can't you do better than that?"

"But it's true."

"And where would this twin sister be at this time?" Steve asked softly.

"She's ill. We were both in an automobile accident several months ago, and though we weren't injured physically, something happened to Carola. She—she had a nervous breakdown, and she's been under treatment by the famous psychologist, Doctor Anton Frejus. We've been staying at his convalescent home, just outside of Las Vegas. I came down with Carola, and I've been with her all the time. It was just today that Doctor Frejus suggested that I take a little time off, and run down into Mexico—"

"Now wait," Steve groaned. "You're going too fast for me. I'm almost beginning to believe you, and that would be pretty bad. I'll swear you sound as if you're telling the truth!"

"It is the truth. Here, let me show you—"

She opened a small locket which hung about her neck, and held it for Steve to look at.

Steve said, "Ouch!" and glanced at Dan Murdoch. Dan shook his head in perplexity. The locket contained a picture of two girls. They were so much alike that it was impossible to tell one from the other—even when side by side, as in the photograph.

"It could be trick photography," Murdoch murmured.

Steve raised his eyes from the locket, to the girl's face. As he looked into her eyes, he could have sworn that he was looking into the eyes of the woman who had aimed the machine gun at him only a short while ago; and who had said so passionately that she hated him, and would like to see him die a dozen deaths.

The girl closed the locket. "But I don't understand," she said bewilderedly. "You—you say that Carola is guilty of espionage, and treason? Carola is in Doctor Frejus's convalescent home, I tell you. She couldn't possibly have been in Mexico tonight!"

"We'll soon find out!" Steve said grimly.

Johnny Kerrigan, at the wheel, said, "Just give me directions for getting to this convalescent home, sister!"

"Turn left on Highway Eleven," she said. "And then left again when we come to the Houston Parkway. It's a half mile off the Parkway."

CHAPTER 4
THE MURDEROUS CANARY

DOCTOR FREJUS'S convalescent home was a hand-some stone structure, set in a beautifully landscaped estate. A gray-haired woman attendant in a spotless white uniform came out upon the portico as the car pulled up the driveway. She stepped over to the car and peered in, and clucked in motherly fashion when she saw the girl.

"I'm so glad you've come back, my dear," she said. "We were all so worried about you. You shouldn't have gone away alone. You know Doctor Frejus doesn't think it safe. It was good of these gentlemen to bring you back." She turned to Johnny Kerrigan.

"I am Doctor Langstrom, the chief assistant to Doctor Frejus. It was really a shock to us to find that Carola had gone off by herself, taking our station wagon."

"Carola?" Johnny repeated sharply.

"But I'm not Carola, Mrs. Langstrom," the girl said swiftly. "I'm Anita."

Mrs. Langstrom gave her a queer look. "Whatever you say, my dear. But come in quickly. The night is so chilly, and you have only your dress on—"

"Do you mind if we all go in?" Steve asked.

Mrs. Langstrom hesitated. "Well, perhaps it would be for the best. Doctor Frejus will want to thank you personally for bringing our patient back."

"But I'm *not* your patient!" the girl exclaimed angrily. "Don't you understand?"

"Of course, my dear," said Mrs. Langstrom. She helped her out of the car. The girl shook her hand off, impatiently. "I can walk by myself—" she began angrily.

She stopped abruptly as Stephen Klaw came up on her other side, and took her other arm.

"Allow me," Steve said grinning. "I'd like to stay close to you—till we find out just who you are!"

The girl's face flushed, but she made no further protest. Kerrigan and Murdoch brought up the rear as they entered the building.

Doctor Frejus's reception room was on the ground floor. He was a portly, bald-headed man of about fifty, with a pair of keen

178

blue eyes. He came over and patted the girl's hand. "My dear, you shouldn't have gone off by yourself."

She snatched her hand away from him. "Will you and Mrs. Langstrom both stop making fools of yourselves? Can't you understand that I'm *not* Carola? What has happened to Carola? Where is she?"

Doctor Frejus looked pained. "Please—don't worry about anything, my dear. Just let Mrs. Langstrom take you upstairs—"

"If you don't mind," Steve interrupted, "we'd just like the young lady to stay here with us—till we get a few things cleared up." As he spoke he flashed his wallet on the doctor, with his F.B.I. identification card.

Frejus raised his eyebrows. "F.B.I.? But why are you interested in this young lady?"

"What about her sister? Which is Carola, and which is Anita?"

"Ah!" said Doctor Frejus. "Perhaps we could talk in private? In my office?"

"Sure," said Steve. He glanced at Dan Murdoch, who nodded. DOCTOR FREJUS led the way into his office. Johnny Kerrigan and Stephen Klaw followed, leaving Murdoch with Mrs. Langstrom and the girl. Once inside, Frejus shut the door, turned, his glance resting on the two men with a professional intentness.

"Gentlemen," he said, "I think I had better tell you the truth in this case. Ethically, I may be wrong, for you understand that these matters are professional secrets. But I feel that under the circumstances I am free to talk to you." He paused, then said slowly, "You see, gentlemen, the fact is—*there is no Carola!*"

"Ah!" said Steve. "And this girl is the Countess Anita Zogc-hinski?"

"That is her name. I have been treating her for a very complicated mental ailment. She did have a twin sister, who was killed in an automobile accident. But Anita believes that her sister is still alive. It is a very serious mental delusion, which may become aggravated in time, if the proper care and treatment is not given. We try to humor her as much as possible, but it is a very difficult situation. Sometimes she becomes almost violent in her demands to see Carola."

"Now look here," Steve said abruptly. "If what you tell us is true, then it was this girl, Anita, who helped to lay a trap for us over the border. It's she who is tied up with one of the deadliest espionage cliques that ever operated in America. It will be our duty to place her under arrest—"

"Good heavens!" Frejus threw up his hands in horror. "That might be fatal to her. It might snap the thin thread that marks the dividing line in her mind between sanity and madness!"

"I'm sorry," said Steve. "There's nothing else we can do—"

He was interrupted by a scream from outside, immediately followed by a crash. Steve and Johnny reached the door together. In the reception room, they saw Dan Murdoch standing before the door of one of the washrooms, pounding on the panel with his fist, and cursing in a low, methodical voice.

"I couldn't go in there with her," he said, "so I let Mrs. Langstrom take her in. Better get around to the outside. I think she's making a break."

Steve and Johnny went racing out to the front entrance, but it was so dark out on the grounds that they couldn't see a thing. They hurried around to the side of the house under the bathroom window. The window was open, and there was a light. Johnny gave Steve a boost up, and he drew himself up to the sill, then climbed in. Anita—or Carola—was not there. But Mrs. Langstrom was groggily picking herself up from the floor. There was a cut in her scalp, and the blood was oozing down along her temple.

"She—she hit me with something from her bag!" Mrs. Langstrom gasped.

Steve made a wry face. He helped her to her feet, and unlocked the door for Murdoch. Then he called down to Kerrigan, "Come on up, Johnny. Our canary is gone!"

CHAPTER 5
DAUGHTER OF DEATH

THE DIRECTOR of the F.B.I. was pacing up and down his office. Every once in a while he would throw a scowl at Johnny Kerrigan and Stephen Klaw.

"The one fault I have to find with you boys is that you go chivalrous on me at the strangest times!"

Steve squirmed in his chair, but didn't say anything.

The Director suddenly smiled. "It's all right, Steve. Don't look so crestfallen. In your place down there in Mexico, I don't think

I'd have brought myself to shoot that woman when she ran away, either. But you shouldn't have lost her. And now you've got to locate her. She's certainly tied up with Blond Otto. Carola or Anita, she'll be a part of whatever Otto has up his sleeve. Otto has the strings of the entire German espionage system in his hands, and if he succeeds in disappearing we'll never know who the Axis agents in this country were. After the war they can just fade back into their former occupations, and go forever unpunished!"

Stephen Klaw stood up. "Murdoch's in New York, sir, working on the Skopa angle. I think Johnny and I ought to go there, too. There's no use our roaming the country in search of that Carola girl—"

"Quite right, Steve. Wherever she is, we'll find her eventually. I've put her on the emergency wanted list, with every field office in the country. And I have that convalescent home of Doctor Frejus under constant observation. We know now that there were two sisters, named Carola and Anita Corbey, and that Anita married a man who called himself Count Ladislas Zogchinski. We also know that Zogchinski has made frequent trips to Mexico, and that he must have been working with Blond Otto. The Polish legation tells us that there is no Zogchinski among the rolls of Polish nobility, so we know that this Count Ladislas Zogchinski must have been an impostor."

"Which all brings us back to the only real lead we have," Steve said. "The lead that Morales kept himself alive to give us."

The Director nodded. "Skopa, of course. Murdoch reports by

phone that he hasn't been able to make contact yet. Better hop a plane, you two, and join him there."

Steve and Johnny arose to go. The chief stopped them at the door. "And remember this—*we want Blond Otto.* We have confidential information that a submarine will try to pick him up somewhere along the coast, and take him back to Germany. We mustn't let him leave!"

Johnny Kerrigan grunted. "If some one will only point him out to us!"

The Director smiled. "That's your job. If we had his description, it would be easy to pick him up. But all we know about him is that he's probably blond, because of his name. We can't go around arresting every blond man in America!"

In the taxi to the airport ten minutes later, Steve and Johnny found themselves looking at every blond-haired man in the street, and wondering if he was Blond Otto. When they boarded the plane, Johnny said, "This is the screwiest business we ever handled, Shrimp. Especially with that girl. Whoever she is, I'd hate to—"

He stopped, swallowed hard, and blinked. Then he nudged Steve violently with his elbow. Up front, in the first seat of the plane, sat a girl. She was talking animatedly, in low tones, with the man at her side. "Shrimp!" Johnny whispered hoarsely. "Do you see what I see?"

"I see it," said Steve. "But I don't believe it."

THE GIRL was Anita—or Carola. There was no doubt of that. Her profile was turned toward them as she talked to the man beside her, and they had an excellent view of the chiseled

183

perfection of her features. She was wearing a heavy fur coat this time, and one of the new military hats with a long visor, trimmed with fur that matched her coat. Underneath the hat, her abundance of black hair was piled high, with wisps showing at the sides. The man to whom she was talking was thin, with a receding chin and sparse, dun-colored hair. He seemed nervous, and kept looking out of the plane window constantly, as if anxious for them to take off.

Johnny Kerrigan scowled, and took a step down the aisle toward the girl, but Steve stopped him.

"Take it easy, Johnny," he said. "As long as she stays on the plane, she can't get away—except by jumping!"

Kerrigan grinned, and slipped into the seat alongside of Steve. The girl kept on talking to her companion, never once looking back at her fellow-passengers. Five minutes later, they got the signal from the control tower, and took off.

The plane was full to capacity, and most of the seats were occupied by men in uniform. They had been up almost an hour, when the dark-haired girl rose from her seat and started to make her way toward the rear. Steve and Johnny immediately buried their heads in their newspapers. Steve was burning to let her look at him, and note her reaction. But he decided that it would be better to remain unnoticed if possible, and tail her and her companion in New York.

The girl did not even glance in their direction when she passed up the aisle. Steve turned his head, and followed her progress. In the bright daylight, she looked much younger than she had looked the night before. She was hardly more than twenty-five or twenty-six. And she certainly didn't seem to be the kind of woman who would train a machine gun on a man and pull the trip with intent to kill. He frowned in perplexity.

Johnny Kerrigan chuckled. "I'd sure like to know if that dame really has a twin sister, or not. If Frejus was telling the truth, she's just plain nuts. But if she was telling the truth, how the devil are we going to know which is which? With two models like that running around loose, we'll be ending up in the nut house!"

"You ought to be thankful," Steve grinned, "that she isn't triplets!"

WHEN THE plane taxied in at the LaGuardia Airport in New York, Johnny and Steve managed to be the first ones out, and hurried across to the administration building and got a taxicab.

"Hold still right here," Steve ordered the driver, showing him his F.B.I. card. "We have a little tailing job to do."

Johnny Kerrigan loitered on the runway, keeping an eye on the passengers, and when he saw the girl coming out with her companion, he hurried into the cab, and they pulled up about fifty feet. Through the rear window they watched their quarry get into another cab.

"Okay," Johnny said to the driver, as he made a note of the other taxi number. "Keep on that cab's tail—like glue!"

The cab they were following swung south to Northern Boulevard, then west toward Manhattan. It crossed the Queensboro Bridge, headed across Sixtieth Street, and stopped for a traffic light at Third Avenue. Johnny and Steve, in the cab behind, were speculating on where the trail would lead, when they saw the door of the other taxi open, and the dark-haired girl get out. She slammed the door and set off at a swift walk up Third Avenue, without turning her head.

"They're splitting!" Steve exclaimed. "I'll take the girl. You follow the man, Johnny!"

"Right, Shrimp!"

Steve opened the door and sprang out, just as the traffic light changed, and the cab ahead moved forward. Steve waved to Johnny, and hurried off up Third Avenue in pursuit of the girl.

She walked two or three blocks north, at a fast pace, without looking behind. Steve kept about fifty feet to the rear, hugging the building line. Suddenly, in the middle of a block, the girl stopped. Steve ducked into a doorway, just as she whirled around to look behind. Steve waited just a moment, then poked his head out. He was just in time to see her disappearing into the doorway of the building in front of which she had stopped. He hurried a little, and came abreast of the house.

It was an old, four-story building, with stores on the street floor, and tenement flats above. On the left hand side of the entrance there was a bar and grille, and on the right side there was a bird store. Steve pushed the entrance door open, and stepped into the hallway of the house. The sudden change from the light in the street to the comparative darkness of the hall-way almost blinded him for an instant, but he stopped short just inside the doorway as the beam of a flashlight flared full in his face, and a gun muzzle was thrust against his ribs.

"Stand still, Stephen Klaw!"

Steve blinked into the light. "Hello, Carola," he said. "Fancy meeting you here!"

"You fool!" she said. "Did you think I hadn't noticed you on the plane? I was hoping it would be you who followed me, and not that partner of yours. I want the satisfaction of killing you. And this time, when I pull the trigger, I shall not miss!"

"Just tell me one thing before you shoot," Steve asked earnestly. "Are there two of you, or just one?"

She laughed bitterly. "Sometimes I don't know, myself."

"Are you Carola? Or Anita?"

"I am both. Sometimes I am Carola, sometimes Anita."

"Well, who are you now?"

"Perhaps when you are dead," she said savagely, "you will know more about such things!" She thrust the revolver muzzle into his ribs. "Walk down the hall slowly."

Steve stared into the bright eye of the flashlight. "If you're going to shoot, why not do it right here? Why walk down the hall?"

"Because I want to take you into a lighted room. I want you to see my face when I shoot you. I want you to know just what it means to be shot down in cold blood!"

HE MOVED down the hall, with her close behind, the muzzle of the gun in his spine, the flashlight bathing him. At the rear of the hall, she ordered, "Go down the cellar stairs!"

Steve pulled open the cellar door. The flashlight from behind him showed a bare and barren cellar, with a furnace and a coal bin, and nothing much else. As he descended slowly, the girl behind him began to speak in a slow, monotonous voice, as if she were repeating something learned a long time ago by rote.

"Do you remember Gaston Zambetta, whom you killed in Valparaiso? Of course you do. You are a killer, and you remember all those men who have died at your hand. I have waited a long time for this moment of revenge, Stephen Klaw. Gaston Zambetta was my father. Now you know why I hate you!"

"Ah!" said Steve, over his shoulder. "Then your name isn't Corbey at all? That was a fairy tale you told me about yourself and your sister? And about Count Ladislas Zogchinski? What about Blond Otto?"

"Through Berlin I was put in touch with him. I undertook to work with him, if he would help me to accomplish my revenge. And at last it has come!" She laughed. "Your man, Murdoch, traced the telephone number that Morales gave you. He is watching the house where Skopa lives, hoping to trap Blond Otto there. But the thing he doesn't know—and the thing that Morales didn't know—*is that Skopa is Blond Otto!*"

"Ah!" said Stephen Klaw.

"So you see," she whispered, "my revenge will be complete. The man who was on the plane with me is a poor fool whom I used as a tool—Ladislas Zogchinski. He will lead your friend Kerrigan a merry chase through the city, while Murdoch watches the house where he expects to trap Blond Otto. But Blond Otto will trap *him* instead! The moment we learned that you had engaged reservations on the plane, we made our plans. Did you think it was coincidence that I was on that plane too?"

She thrust the gun harder into Steve's spine. "Go down those stairs! And remember that I am behind you."

Slowly, Steve began to descend. Behind him, he heard her take one step, then another. The light was still bathing him, throwing its eerie glare down into the cellar. Steve tensed. He could almost sense that the woman's finger was tightening on the trigger, that in a moment she would send a slug into his spine. He waited for a fraction of a second more, timing himself with instinctive accuracy; and then he suddenly leaped forward, straight out into the air!

Behind him, he heard the spiteful crack of the woman's gun as she fired. He couldn't have timed his jump better if he had been able to read her mind.

THE BULLET whined past him as he hurtled through the air. He landed on the cellar floor on his feet, bending his knees with the resiliency of a cat to take up the shock of the landing. A second shot cracked, and the bullet ploughed into the cement floor at his feet. Above him, he heard the woman's scream of hate and balked vengeance, as she fired a third time.

Steve's hands were already in his pockets, gripping his two automatics. He had the muzzles angling upward, and he had only to pull the triggers to fire through the cloth of his pockets and send a hail of slugs into her body.

But once again, as at that squalid hovel in Mexico, something indefinable stayed his hand. Inherently, Stephen Klaw was one who admired and appreciated the ultimate things in life. Perhaps it was her beauty, perhaps the justness—from her point of view—of her hatred of him. Even at the cost of his life, Stephen Klaw hesitated.

And then the hand of fate intervened. Carola in her eagerness leaned too far forward on the top step in order to aim better, and lost her balance. She uttered a sharp, startled cry, and toppled forward, coming down the stairs in a tangle of arms and legs, the gun flying out of her grasp. Three times her head struck the edge of the stairs in that ghastly fall, and as she landed on the concrete cellar floor there was a wicked *thud*, and she lay still, almost at Stephen Klaw's feet, with her head twisted at a strange and unnatural angle. Her neck had been broken—

Stephen Klaw stood looking down at the broken body of the beautiful woman who had planned his destruction so carefully—only to be defeated by her own vengefulness. Suddenly, his eyes narrowed, as he glimpsed a small packet which had dropped from her bodice as she fell. He stooped and picked it up. It consisted of half a dozen sheets of the thinnest onion-skin paper, upon which were traced a series of complicated designs and figures.

Klaw studied them under the light for a moment, and gasped. He recognized them as a complete set of plans of the newest tank which had been put in production for the army—the General Lafayette. It was a tank which not a dozen men in the country knew about, for it was being built for a specific attack purpose, and its construction would give away the neat large-scale United Nations attack on the global front. Advance information regarding them, would enable the enemy not only to prepare against them—but would also tell the leaders of the Axis from what quarter to expect attack!

CHAPTER 6
"YOU ARE CAROLA..."

STEPHEN KLAW left without waiting for the police. He found his way out through the rear door of the cellar, and five minutes later he was in a telephone booth, urgently phoning the New York Field Office of the F.B.I. In his haste, the few seconds he had to wait seemed as many hours.

"Prentice?" he said to the Agent at the other end. "What's the address of that Quincy phone number that Dan Murdoch is casing? Give it to me quick, and don't ask any questions!"

"The Savonarola Apartments," Prentice told him. "On West End Avenue. Apartment 9C. What's up?"

"They're about to reverse the trap on Dan," Steve said.

He hung up and dashed out and got a taxi. Ten minutes later, he was piling out at the corner of the block on which the Savonarola Apartments were located. He didn't waste time reconnoitering the place. Prentice had given him the apartment number—9C. He knew where he had to go, but he wanted to make sure, first, that Murdoch wasn't on the outside. He didn't see Murdoch—but his eyes widened when he spotted Johnny Kerrigan getting out of a taxicab right in front of the Savona-rola. He came running up to the cab, just in time to see Johnny hauling out a wilted man, by a wilted collar. The other was the man they had been tailing—Ladislas Zogchinski.

Johnny saw Steve coming, and grinned. "This bird kept riding around town without getting anywhere, so it dawned on me he was giving me a runaround. You know I don't like runarounds, Steve, so I got into his cab and had a little session with him, and he opened up and told me where to find Skopa—"

Johnny's face clouded as Steve told him what he'd learned and ended with, "I'm afraid that Dan is up there—in a jam."

"Well, what are we waiting for?" Johnny growled. He lifted his prisoner up by the collar. "Just to keep you safe, friend," he said, and tapped him on the jaw. The man went limp, and Johnny dropped him back on to the floor of the cab. He winked at the driver. "Just keep a watch on our friend, will you? I doubt if he'll start coming to, but if he should, just tap him again with a monkey wrench!"

The driver grinned. "For the F.B.I.—it'll be a pleasure!"

THE ELEVATOR boy took a set of passkeys from his pocket, and handed them over. "This key will open the door," he said. "But you want to watch yourself. I always thought there was something fishy about that joint. There's a lot of men always go in there, but I never see many of them come out. They must use the service elevator. It's rented in the name of a Mr. Skopa, but I never see him. And the super tells me the rent is always paid in cash, not by check. It's sent here by messenger boy—"

"When you see the super," Kerrigan said drily, "tell him he'll have an apartment to rent from the first of next month!"

At the ninth, Johnny and Steve left the elevator, telling the boy to get his cage down to the main floor, and not to come up unless he got a three-five signal ring.

"If you get that ring from this floor," Johnny told him, "come up. But if you get any other ring, it'll mean we're dead. In that case, you scram out to the nearest phone, and call the F.B.I. Tell them to send a riot car over, and to shoot to kill!"

They moved down the corridor to Nine C, and stopped before the door.

"If Dan is in there," said Johnny Kerrigan, "he certainly isn't making much fuss!" He took out both his heavy revolvers.

Steve Klaw stepped up close with the passkey, inserted it in the lock, and turned, slowly and carefully. Then he twisted the knob, and thrust the door wide open, with a swift shove. Johnny Kerrigan, with both revolvers pointing ahead of him, went through the open doorway like an avalanche. Klaw followed, drawing both automatics.

They both stopped short just inside the foyer, their eyes narrowing. There were only three people in the living room. One was Doctor Frejus, the other was Mrs. Langstrom, his assistant at the Frejus Convalescent Home. But it was the third person at whom they both stared, unbelievingly. It was a woman. She was sitting upright in a straight-backed chair, and her upper body was tightly bound in an ugly-looking, white strait-jacket, tightened to the cruelest limit.

Looking at her face, Steve sucked his breath in, sharply; because she was a dead ringer for that other beautiful woman whom he had just left for dead with a broken neck, in the cellar of that house on Third Avenue. There was a vicious gag in her mouth, making it impossible for her to speak, but her eyes were brilliantly alive with an urgency which would not be denied.

Doctor Frejus's mouth dropped open at sight of Kerrigan and Klaw. Mrs. Langstrom uttered a little gasp of surprise. Immediately, however, Doctor Frejus recovered control of himself, and a broad smile lit up his gaunt face. He took a step forward.

"Mr. Klaw! And Mr. Kerrigan! This is indeed a surprise!"

Stephen Klaw moved into the room, and went swiftly to the other doors, peering into each of the other rooms, making sure that there was no one else in the apartment. Then he returned to the living room. Johnny Kerrigan had remained at his post, covering Doctor Frejus and Mrs. Langstrom.

"Really, gentlemen," said Doctor Frejus, with a hurt expression, "your guns are unnecessary. I am sure you don't suspect me of any crime—"

"Let's skip the honey and oil," Steve Klaw said drily. "Where's Dan Murdoch?"

"Murdoch? I'm sure I haven't seen him—"

"You lie!"

Frejus's eyes became veiled and cunning. "But Mr. Klaw—"

"Never mind that line. We know Dan Murdoch came up here. What are you and Mrs. Langstrom doing here?"

"WE ONLY came to find poor Anita, here. We were informed that she had come to this place, and we flew up to take her back with us to Texas. But she became violent, and we were compelled to place her in a strait-jacket."

"Sure, sure," said Steve. "And what about the other one—Carola?"

"But I told you, Mr. Klaw, that there is no other one. Carola died many months ago."

Klaw gestured impatiently. He strode over and grasped hold of Frejus's lapels, in one hand. *"Are you going to tell us where Dan Murdoch is?"*

The other did not answer.

Klaw thrust Frejus savagely back into a corner, and swung around. Johnny Kerrigan was already working at the fastenings of the strait-jacket which bound Anita Zogchinski. As soon as he got it loose, he helped her out of it, and removed the gag. For a few moments she was numb from lack of circulation, but she managed to speak.

"Your friend, Murdoch, has walked into a trap! I've—just found out that—Carola—has been working with these spies. It was she who arranged the trap for Murdoch. And—and I understood that she had arranged for your deaths—"

"She did," Steve said drily. "But something slipped."

Anita's eyes widened. "What—what happened to her?"

Klaw put a hand on her shoulder. "Your sister is dead!" he said softly.

Anita buried her head in her hands. She sat that way for a moment, then raised her eyes to Steve's. "Perhaps it is better that way. I—I was raised here in America. Gaston Zambetta was my father, but I bore no ill-will to those who had brought him to justice, for I knew the kind of work he had been engaged in. But Carola was different. She was brought up in Italy, and she imbibed Fascist doctrines since she was a baby. She—she held it against me that I didn't want to work against those who—killed father. When she heard of our father's death, she swore vengeance on the Suicide Squad, and she has worked with Blond Otto for that one purpose, ever since!"

"What about Frejus here?"

Anita's eyes flashed fire. "Frejus and Mrs. Langstrom are agents of Blond Otto. They've been feeding me drugs, so that I'd feel weak and ill, ever since that auto accident. They told me that Carola had been killed in that accident, but she wasn't. They were only nursing me along, so that when the proper time came, they could blame whatever Carola did, on me. I never suspected a thing till I got here. I heard the plans of Blond Otto, and tried to get away, but they caught me and gagged me and put me in that terrible strait-jacket!"

"Then you know what's happened to Dan Murdoch?" Klaw asked eagerly.

She nodded. "Skopa had been posing as a weak rat, ready to squeal. But in reality, he's nothing of the sort. He's really the Hangman!"

"Yes." said Stephen Klaw. "I know that. It proves that you're telling the truth."

"Murdoch came here an hour ago," she hurried on. "They had me in the strait-jacket in the next room, and I heard everything that went on, but I was gagged, and couldn't warn Murdoch. Skopa told Murdoch that he would take him to the secret hiding place of Blond Otto, and Murdoch rose to the bait. He went with Skopa."

"Where?"

"I don't know."

JOHNNY KERRIGAN swung on Frejus. "You're going

to talk, Doc! You're going to tell us where to find Murdoch!" His eyes were blazing as he strode toward Frejus, and the man cowered back from him.

"I swear to you I don't know! I was never taken into Blond Otto's confidence."

Kerrigan smiled coldly, and seized him by the throat. His two great hands contracted on the man's windpipe.

But Anita exclaimed, "It's true, Mr. Kerrigan, he doesn't know any more than I do. I heard them talking. They never told Frejus much. They wouldn't trust him with the secret of Blond Otto's real hiding place!"

Slowly, Johnny Kerrigan's mighty hands relaxed their grip on the purple-faced man's throat. Frejus sank down to the floor, gasping for breath. Mrs. Langstrom sat, white-faced, like a frozen image.

Johnny Kerrigan looked hopelessly at Stephen Klaw. "We're at a dead end, Shrimp. Dan is walking into a death trap, and we're helpless to spring him out of it!"

Klaw was biting his nether lip. "Try to think of everything that happened while you were listening in the next room," he urged Anita. "Maybe some little thing that took place will give us a clue."

"There was nothing much," Anita said slowly, "except for one telephone call from Carola. It was before Murdoch came. From what Blond Otto said at this end, it seems that Carola has obtained possession of certain information about the new General Lafayette tanks, being manufactured for the American army. There are half a dozen German tank officers in Blond

Otto's secret hiding place, who have been smuggled into this country. Carola will give them the information, and they will return to Germany to assume command of special tank-destroyer units. With the special knowledge gained from Carola, they expect to develop new methods of combating the General Lafayettes."

Steve looked thoughtful. In his pocket were the plans which had fallen from the bodice of Carola when she landed at the foot of those cellar steps. These then, were the plans which were to instruct Blond Otto's men!

Anita said, "I wasn't able to hear everything, but I gathered that Carola was leading you and Mr. Kerrigan into a trap, and was then coming to meet Blond Otto and give the lecture to the tank men. Blond Otto said that he had changed his secret headquarters, and that he would have one of his men meet Carola in front of Grand Central Station, and conduct her to the headquarters—"

"Hold everything!" shouted Stephen Klaw, his eyes glittering. His gaze met that of Johnny Kerrigan, and there was suppressed excitement in the look of both of them. Steve swung back to Anita. "You say that Blond Otto is sending a man to meet Carola and conduct her to the secret headquarters—"

She nodded. "At ten o'clock—she was to bring the plans—"

Steve glanced swiftly at his watch. It was nine-forty-five. He snatched out the tank plans and thrust them into Anita's hand. "Blond Otto doesn't know yet that your sister is dead. *You* are going to be Carola tonight!"

CHAPTER 7
GHOST GUNS

AT THE stroke of ten, the lithe, beautiful figure of Anita Zogchinski stood at the curb in front of Grand Central Station. Even Stephen Klaw, watching her, could not be absolutely sure which one of the two it was who lay dead and undiscovered in the cellar of that squalid house on Third Avenue. That one had said that she was Carola; this one said that she was Anita. But suppose they both had lied? Suppose they both were enlisted in the ranks of Blond Otto—suppose that Anita was playing an elaborate hoax which would lead Johnny Kerrigan and Stephen Klaw to their deaths!

Neither Kerrigan nor Klaw cared much, either way. They knew only that Dan Murdoch was in a trap, and that they must reach him somehow. If at the price of their own lives—well, that was part of the game; a game they played for the highest stakes imaginable.

It was at one minute and six seconds after ten o'clock by Kerrigan's wrist watch when they saw the hansom cab draw up at the curb in front of the spot where Anita stood. One man alone sat in the enclosed section underneath, while the coachman up above sat smartly erect, in his tall top hat.

"Well, I'll be damned!" said Johnny Kerrigan. "Blond Otto certainly sends for his women in style!"

Hansom cabs are no novelty to New Yorkers who frequent Central Park, for there, in that spot of beauty amid the man-made forest of tall buildings, has been preserved one of the delightful old customs of nineteenth century New York. But many people often turn to look at these vehicles, and it was eloquent testimony to the cunning shrewdness of Blond Otto that he should have dared to send such a conspicuous conveyance to conduct Carola to his secret rendezvous—by its very daring, the act dispelled suspicion.

For Kerrigan and Klaw, however, it made the task of tailing a bit easier. They had no difficulty in following the hansom on its leisurely course across town, and up Fifth Avenue. In fact, their cab driver was put to it to keep his taxi down to the comparative snail's pace.

And then Johnny Kerrigan swore abruptly, as he realized Blond Otto's strategy. At one of the transverse cuts which conducted traffic across town through the park, the hansom turned off, with the tailing cab a hundred feet behind. On the long straightaway, the creeping cab would be a dead giveaway to the hansom's occupants, that they were being followed—Blond Otto had chosen his vehicle even more shrewdly than Kerrigan and Klaw had guessed!

At Johnny's orders, the cab driver fell even farther behind. Halfway through the park, the road turned in a sharp curve; and when they came around the curve, they glimpsed the hansom once more. It was Stephen Klaw who first realized that the vehicle was empty!

They sent their cab urgently alongside, and both men sprang out of the taxi and called to the coachman. Steve showed his F.B.I. card. "The man and woman you were driving—where are they?"

THE COACHMAN'S face whitened. "They paid me off, and jumped out, just as we rounded the curve back there. They said they wanted to stroll through the park—"

Neither Johnny or Steve waited to hear any more. Grimly, they set off at a swift run, back toward that spot. Their eyes were bleak and hard as they ran. They had been tricked—whether with or without Anita's consent, they didn't know. But the fact remained that if they lost Anita they lost their only chance of locating the headquarters of Blond Otto, and of springing Dan Murdoch from the Nazi's trap.

They reached the curve in the road, and stopped, looking around hopelessly. On either side, the high wall of the transverse precluded the possibility that Anita or her companion could have climbed up into the park. But set into the wall of the transverse there were three doors, which, they knew, led to the storage chambers of the City Park Department. It was here that the Park Department stored the tractors and implements used for keeping the grounds in order. But of late, due to the curtailment of machinery manufacture, two of the underground storerooms had been abandoned.

Johnny tried one of the doors, and Steve the other. They were both locked.

"The chances are ten to one," Johnny said, "that they've—"

Just then, Steve grasped Kerrigan's arm. "Take a look, Mope!"

Another hansom was coming down the transverse. There were two men in it, and one of them was leaning out in order to speak to the coachman. In response to the order, the coachman began to rein in the horse.

"Let's duck, Shrimp!" exclaimed Johnny. They streaked for the third door, that of the storeroom still in use, pushed it open, and slipped inside, just as the hansom cab came to a stop. Holding the door open a crack, Steve saw the two men alight, pay off the coachman, and stand there until the hansom pulled out of sight. Then one of them looked up and down to make sure there were no other vehicles approaching, while the other stepped up to one of the two doors, and inserted a key. He opened the door without difficulty, called to the other gutturally, and his companion hurried over to join him. The two men slipped inside.

But Kerrigan and Klaw were already streaking out of their hiding place. They hit the door just as it was closing, and their combined weight sent it slamming inward, throwing both of the strange men in a heap on the floor. Klaw drew his gun.

Johnny turned and swung the door shut, locking it from the inside, while Steve knelt down and removed the two men's belts and bound their arms tightly with them, then gagged them with their handkerchiefs and neckties.

That done, the two of them studied the store room.

"I'm thinking," Johnny said, "that we shouldn't have hit these two guys so hard. If they're Blond Otto's men, on their way to a meeting in the secret headquarters, they know how to get in. But they'll be in no condition to talk for a while—"

Steve was feeling along the walls, and Johnny joined him. It was Johnny who discovered that the innocent looking electric-lamp cord hanging from the ceiling was really the switch they sought. He yanked hard on it, and it descended a couple of inches. At the same time, a section of one wall swung open noiselessly, on well-oiled hinges.

They approached the opening revealed by the moving panel. There was a narrow corridor beyond it, and Steve led the way, with Johnny close behind. The corridor turned sharply at the end of about ten feet, and they saw that light was reflected from somewhere around the turn. They moved forward, then made the turn, and stopped, staring up into a vaulted chamber.

It was a strange sight that met their gaze.

DAN MURDOCH was seated on a bench, twiddling his thumbs. Behind him stood a small blond man with a sub-machine gun in the crook of his arm. At one end of the room there was a blackboard, and at the other there were two long benches facing the blackboard. Upon the benches were seated a dozen men, watching Anita draw figures on the blackboard.

She was copying them from the plans which Steve had given her, and her face was set and desperate.

The blond man, looking down sardonically at Murdoch, was speaking. "As soon as Carola is finished with the lecture, Mr. Murdoch, we shall have the pleasure of wiping you out. It will comfort you in your last moments, to know that your two partners are already dead, and that these men who are listening to this lecture will be back in Germany within two weeks, with the latest secrets of your newest tanks in their heads, prepared to wipe them out when they appear upon the battlefield!"

But Anita, at the blackboard suddenly exclaimed, "No, no! I won't let it happen!" Abruptly, she began to tear up the plans. She tore them to bits, and scattered them in the air.

Blond Otto scowled. "Carola! Have you gone mad? What does this mean?"

She was glorious in her defiance as she stood before the blackboard, her dark eyes flashing. And Murdoch's eyes, too, lit up with sudden exhilaration.

"I think, Shrimp," Johnny Kerrigan called loudly from the doorway, "that this is our entrance cue!"

And the two of them stepped into the room, still shoulder to shoulder.

Blond Otto heard that stentorian voice of Johnny Kerrigan's. He uttered a cry of rage, and swung the muzzle of the machine-gun toward the doorway.

Johnny Kerrigan and Stephen Klaw grinned with pleasure, and each of them fired once. The two slugs almost met in the center of Blond Otto's forehead.

The shots were still re-echoing in the room as the men seated on the benches sprang up, drawing weapons from their pockets. But Dan Murdoch, moving now with the swift and deadly lithe-ness of a panther, had leaped forward and caught the machine gun from the already-dead hands of Blond Otto. He swung it to cover those Nazi tank experts, and they—losing all interest in a losing fight—hastily raised their hands in the air.

Murdoch turned and winked at Steve and Johnny. "Come in, you guys. You're the most welcome ghosts I've seen. Blond Otto had you both nicely butchered, and on ice. I never thought I'd enjoy another drink with you two, again!"

Johnny grinned. "Speaking of drinks, you *do* get a good idea once in a while."

Stephen Klaw went over to Anita, who was leaning against the blackboard, weak from the reaction of the last few fiery moments. He smiled, and took her arm. "We'll drink to you, Anita," he told her softly. "To the bravest girl we've met!"

She smiled, and swallowed hard. "Coming from the Suicide Squad," she said, "that's the sweetest compliment I've ever heard!"